"I can't get you out of my mind, Kelly," Garth said. "I tried. I really tried. But I can't do it."

She couldn't bear his scrutiny another second. She spun, panicking, but she couldn't convince her traitorous legs to take her out of his house and away from him.

"I see you, feel you, taste you in my dreams," came his soft, husky voice dangerously close to her ear. Then his fingers touched her neck, pushing back her hair and brushing fire across her skin.

"Oh, Garth—" she whispered.

"I know you're scared." He trailed his hand down along her shoulder, prodding her to face him. "I'm scared too."

She turned and he touched her cheek with a tender stroke before dropping his hand to his side.

"You are?" She stared up at him.

"Scared to death," he admitted. "What I'm feeling right now is so powerful that I can't eat or sleep or breathe without thinking of you. I know we said we should keep our distance, but I can't. . . ."

# WHAT ARE *LOVESWEPT* ROMANCES?

*They are stories of true romance and touching emotion. We believe those two very important ingredients are constants in our highly sensual and very believable stories in the LOVE-SWEPT line. Our goal is to give you, the reader, stories of consistently high quality that may sometimes make you laugh, sometimes make you cry, but are always fresh and creative and contain many delightful surprises within their pages.*

*Most romance fans read an enormous number of books. Those they truly love, they keep. Others may be traded with friends and soon forgotten. We hope that each LOVESWEPT romance will be a treasure—a "keeper." We will always try to publish*

## LOVE STORIES YOU'LL NEVER FORGET
## BY AUTHORS YOU'LL ALWAYS REMEMBER

*The Editors*

*Loveswept* ®897

# UNDENIABLE

## SUZANNE McMINN

**BANTAM BOOKS**
*NEW YORK · TORONTO · LONDON · SYDNEY · AUCKLAND*

UNDENIABLE

*A Bantam Book / July 1998*

ISBN 0-553-44636-3

*Published simultaneously in the United States and Canada*

*Bantam Books are published by Bantam Books, a division of Bantam Dou-
bleday Dell Publishing Group, Inc. Its trademark, consisting of the words
"Bantam Books" and the portrayal of a rooster, is Registered in U.S. Patent
and Trademark Office and in other countries. Marca Registrada. Bantam
Books, 1540 Broadway, New York, New York 10036.*

PRINTED IN THE UNITED STATES OF AMERICA

OPM    10 9 8 7 6 5 4 3 2 1

For my precious princess, my daughter Morgan. Although I was already the mother of two wonderful sons, my heart still ached for a daughter—so much so that I dreamed up a book about a character with *four* daughters! Now Morgan and the book are both dreams come true. For the book, I thank my editor, Joy Abella, and my agent, Pam Hopkins. For my little girl, I thank my husband, Gerald, and God.

# ONE

Kelly Thompson lifted her head slightly and with one cautious finger pushed on the lid of her coffin. Her ears immediately picked up on the *slap-slap* of little feet. She peeked out through the sliver-thin opening and caught a flash of something white.

A little ghost? A tiny angel?

She didn't wait to see. Dropping the lid shut, she smiled to herself and waited as the customary thrill of this special night raced through her veins.

The sounds came closer, the soft rustling of costumes was accompanied by laughing voices. Apparently, there was more than one visitor. Kelly's smile broadened. The more the merrier.

She prepared herself for the moment she would briefly escape the suffocating blackness of the coffin. A blackness made bearable only by how much fun she had each time she popped out.

Luckily, the temperature was relatively warm

for late October in Texas. The night air held only the slightest nip. Perfect.

The high-pitched voices quieted suddenly, and she knew her resting place had been discovered.

"Look!" one cried. Kelly imagined the little speaker pointing to the coffin.

"What's that?" a second one asked.

"Creepy! Do you think it's for real?" the first one questioned. "Do you think somebody's in there?"

A deep male voice broke into the babble. "Come back over here, girls. Of course nobody's in there."

Kelly held her breath. She didn't want to give away the game at this point.

"Come on," the man said.

She imagined him herding the little owners of the two voices back together. The sound of a firm knock followed.

This was it! It was time.

Kelly pushed up on the lid of the coffin slowly, letting the unoiled hinges creak and groan. She had the act down pat after all these years.

A chorus of gasps fell over the front porch as Kelly rose to a sitting position and faced her visitors. She knew she looked a sight with long black hair, specter-white face, bloodred lips, and body encased in a sable-colored sheath.

Three little ghosts met her eyes, not two. Kelly held out a big bowl of candy to the trio waiting on her doorstep.

"Would you like a treat?" she said, using her best Vampira imitation and struggling to maintain a properly ghoulish composure. She loved Halloween.

Hesitantly, the biggest ghost started toward the dim corner of the porch, where Kelly waited. The middle-size ghost followed.

The littlest ghost screamed.

The man suddenly stepped out of the evening's dusk and into the golden spill of porchlight beside the door. He scooped the tiny, screaming child into his arms and glared at Kelly.

"Are you crazy?" he ground out. "My daughter's three years old. What are you trying to do? Scare her to death?"

From where Kelly sat in her coffin, the man appeared huge—at least ten feet tall.

She knew she was being silly, but she felt like a tiny speck in comparison.

The two ghosts left standing on the porch remained rooted in place, their white sheets swaying around their ankles. Their arms poked out of holes on each side, allowing them to carry their goody bags. Their eyes, revealed by circular cutouts, shifted back and forth between the enticing candy in Kelly's bowl and the man's angry scowl. The smallest ghost clutched at him, burrowing into his shoulder, goody bag gripped in a fist.

"No, of course not! I . . . I was just . . ." Kelly stammered out an explanation. She'd never had this reaction before!

She was famous in her Hope, Texas, neighborhood for her Halloween trick. She loved playing the creepy ghoul rising from a homemade, painted wooden casket to offer up Halloween treats. The children always loved it too.

"She's shaking, for crying out loud!" The man hugged his child and cut another black look at Kelly. "It's okay, Toby," he whispered, his dark eyes softening as he looked down at his daughter. "It's okay."

Kelly's pulse jagged into an uncomfortable rhythm for a few seconds. She felt a tiny swirl of warmth in her stomach as she witnessed the obvious love of a father for his child. Then the man turned his eyes back to meet hers. They were icy, and all her warm feelings froze.

If looks could kill, Kelly thought glumly, she'd need this coffin for real.

"I didn't mean to scare her like that," she said. She frowned. No, that wasn't quite right. "I mean, I *was* trying to scare her," she had to admit. "But not like that. Not in a bad way."

The man's scowl deepened. Apparently, he had no sense of humor. He made her feel like a toad. Kelly swung her legs over the side of the coffin and, hefting the large bowl of candy, stood.

Stretched to her full height, she met his glare squarely and discovered that the man was still huge, though not so mythically tall as he'd first appeared. At five-nine, she was above-average height herself, so she guessed him to be well over six feet—easily intimidation-level.

She felt herself shrinking—a reaction to which, she thought, he was probably accustomed. Not only did he possess overwhelming height, he was a looker, to boot.

She could guess what charm he might exude if he smiled. Well, she doubted she'd have a chance to find out, the way things were going.

Not that she wanted to know. She didn't. She was free. Free! And this was hardly the time for new attachments.

But neither did she want to make enemies.

"Look, I really do apologize," Kelly offered. "If there's anything I can do . . ." Her words trailed off helplessly.

The man made no move to accept her apology. She found irritation lacing its way up her spine.

Who did this guy think he was, anyway?

A quick glance at the two older children told her that they weren't scared of her in the least. In fact, they were craning their necks trying to check out the coffin behind her.

Even the ghost in her father's arms was now peeking out, face half turned toward Kelly, eyes cautiously curious. Kelly tried smiling at her, but the child quickly hid her face in her father's neck again.

To Kelly, she looked more shy than scared.

"Don't be scared, sweetheart," she said reassuringly. She wished she could reach out and pat the little girl on the back, but the look on the father's face stopped her cold. Little Toby peeked at her again, not hiding her face this time when Kelly smiled. Still, she kept a tight grip on her father.

Kelly settled for gaining that much ground. Turning to the older girls, she grinned. "You're not scared of me, are you?"

They shook their heads.

"Want to look in my coffin?" Kelly asked.

They nodded their heads and scampered over.

Kelly looked back at the children's father. "See, this is all in fun—"

"Well, maybe you should put up a warning sign next year," the man cut in, not one whit less testy than he'd been before.

Kelly bristled. "Well, maybe *you* shouldn't be taking a three-year-old out on Halloween if you don't think she's ready," she shot back. "I do this every year. And I've never gotten this sort of response before. If I had, I wouldn't do it."

She stopped, struggling to keep herself from becoming any angrier than she already was. She didn't want to upset the children by getting into a full-blown argument in front of them.

It was a pity the little tyke was so timid. Kelly wished she could make her feel more comfortable. Not that the overprotective brute was likely to let her try.

"The neighborhood kids would be disappointed if I didn't do this," she continued coolly. "They love it—"

"Well, not these neighborhood kids."

Kelly blinked. She was so stunned by the implication that he lived in the neighborhood that she forgot to point out that at least two of his kids were perfectly fascinated with her Halloween setup.

"You live around here?" she asked.

She'd never seen the man in front of her, she was certain of that. With his dark visage, arrow-sharp eyes, and intimidating height, she wouldn't have forgotten him if she'd ever met him.

Ignoring her, the man shifted the child in his arms to his hip and with his free hand shooed the other girls ahead of him toward the steps of the wooden porch. "Come on, Carrie, Michelle. Let's go."

"But, Daddy . . ." the older children whined in unison, their eyes on the candy bowl in Kelly's arms.

"There are plenty of other houses in the neighborhood." He prodded them onward. "You'll get your candy." He didn't look at Kelly again. He nudged the children off the porch.

Leaning against a post, confused, Kelly stared after them as they disappeared into the dark.

"Not these neighborhood kids," he'd railed at her. Kelly knew everybody in the neighborhood. Heck, she knew practically every person in the small north Texas town of Hope.

She returned to the coffin, still bewildered. She could hear other children coming up the street, children who no doubt expected their yearly Halloween spooking at the Thompson house.

Kelly couldn't let them down. She lowered the coffin lid once again, clutching the candy bowl against her stomach, determined to do it right.

She'd taken over the Thompson Halloween tradition from her parents when they'd died six years earlier—along with other, heavier responsibilities, such as raising her twelve-year-old twin siblings. Now that Brian and Bethany were finally off to college, she supposed she could have let the holiday spooking lapse, especially since she'd arrived home just a few hours ago.

She'd been gone all week, relaxing on the Mexican Riviera courtesy of a free airline ticket and half-price luxury-hotel accommodations. The vacation was thanks to her longtime job with Holiday World Travel, one of quaint Hope's two travel agencies. For a small town, Holiday World did a brisk business, and in the past Kelly had passed up many opportunities for free or nearly free travel.

Brian and Bethany were now ensconced in their own apartment in Lubbock, busy with college, new friends, and their futures, while Kelly, at twenty-seven, was finally free to do the things she'd only dreamed about during the past six years. The things she'd given up at the age of twenty-one, when she'd become the legal guardian of two frightened, grief-stricken children.

She planned to spend as much time as she could traveling, starting with little weekend jaunts planned throughout the fall and a Christmas Caribbean cruise with several of her single friends. Now that Brian and Bethany were old enough to make their own holiday plans—skiing with friends during their winter break—Kelly was free to indulge herself.

Even so, there were certain things about Hope that she treasured, and Halloween was one of them. And so she'd rushed home from the airport, and just before dusk she had hauled the old casket out onto the porch.

Her first experience that evening had put a damper on her fun, but she wasn't going to let some uptight father ruin it.

Fortunately, she'd seen the last of him, and good riddance, she decided. Whatever his problem was, she didn't have to worry about it. She took a deep breath, then expelled the bad feelings her encounter with the man had engendered.

Then sudden, stark realization zipped into Kelly's consciousness, catching her unawares. She gasped and started to sit up in surprised reaction, smacking her forehead against the closed lid. Biting back a yelp of discomfort, she knew with a sinking feeling in her belly exactly who she'd just alienated.

She knew another thing too. She hadn't seen the last of him. Not by a long shot.

◆───────◆

"Want one of my lollipops, Daddy?"

Garth Holloway smiled tiredly. He gave up his search for a spatula, set aside the still-packed box of kitchen utensils he was sifting through, and sat down across the table from his youngest daughter.

Breakfast and unpacking could wait. Toby needed him now.

"Sure, sweetie." He accepted Toby's offering, knowing she would be disappointed if he didn't. Despite the casual eating habits he'd let them all slide into during the past week, he didn't typically indulge her, or himself, in candy before breakfast.

He let the nutrition lecture go for now. Toby had already experienced enough of the world's hard realities for a three-year-old.

Garth squeezed his eyes shut against the sudden pain that swamped him at the thought of his daughter's hurt. Who was he kidding? She'd known enough pain for an entire lifetime. All of them had.

"It's a grape one. Grape's my favorite. Is it your favorite, Daddy?"

Garth opened his eyes, mentally shaking himself. It was easy, too easy, to let his mood turn black these days. For the kids' sake, if for nothing else, he had to pretend their world hadn't been smashed like a soda can that had been run over by a Mack truck.

"I love grape," he affirmed. Toby smiled, her round cherub's face lighting up as she turned her full attention to her sticky lollipop.

She was fragile right now. They all were. Fortunately, Toby had gotten over seeing their next-door neighbor rise out of a coffin.

A little streak of guilt tugged at Garth's gut. He knew that he'd probably come down too hard on the woman. As a kid, he would have gotten a real kick out of her spooky setup.

He just hadn't been expecting it. It had been a long, emotional week that had begun with saying good-bye to the Dallas home he'd bought ten years earlier, when he still thought forever meant just that.

They were starting over now—a new town, a new home, a new life. He had everyone enrolled in their new schools, even little Toby. She would be attending an excellent preschool right across the street from the Hope Animal Clinic, where Garth was joining an already thriving practice. He had the plan all worked out, ready to be put into action first thing Monday morning. The high school let out first, so Liza would be home in time to greet and watch over Carrie and Michelle. By five, Garth would pick up Toby. He hoped he would figure out how to cook before they all starved—the housekeeper he'd hired after Julia left had declined to follow the family into what she'd groused were the "sticks."

With all the changes going on, Garth had hoped that taking the kids trick-or-treating would help them better acclimate to their new environment. Liza had refused to emerge from her new room to accompany her sisters, however, and Toby had been sniffling before they'd even left the house. She'd been crying on and off all afternoon for "Toby's house," meaning their old house. Only Carrie and Michelle had seemed in the spirit of the evening.

Unfortunately, at the first house they'd visited, their neighbor had startled Toby. So the poor woman had been on the receiving end of all the frustration and repressed emotion of the past week.

A rather pretty "poor woman" at that—a fact that, he had to admit, might have had a little something to do with his overreaction. He'd found the woman attractive the instant she'd risen out of her creepy casket. Beneath the ghastly white paint, ruby-red lipstick, and a wig that would have done Elvira proud, she possessed small, fine features. And that black thing she'd been wearing hadn't done much to hide her slender curves either. His instinctive male response had been a lot scarier than any Halloween trick.

He'd thought he had that part of himself on ice. Permanently. Discovering it was dormant, not dead, was not a happy revelation.

Equally unwanted was the nudge from his conscience telling him he owed the woman an apology. The last thing he wanted was to face her again. Developing even a nodding acquaintance with an attractive neighbor definitely was *not* on his to-do list.

He didn't need that kind of trouble.

A cabinet door banged suddenly, capturing Garth's attention. He knew that bang even before he turned his head. Liza was still mad.

"Hey, Liza."

She didn't respond. Presenting her back to her father, her waist-long bouncy blond hair swaying, she flipped on the kitchen faucet. She filled a plastic cup decorated with cartoon characters, one of the few items that had been put away.

"Look, Liza!" Toby cried. "Look at all my candy!"

Liza turned and looked at the pile of Halloween candy Toby had dumped out of her goody bag onto the center of the kitchen table. Having remained holed up in her room even after her sisters had returned the night before, Liza had yet to hear about their adventures.

"Uh-huh" was all Toby got out of her sister.

"You should have come with us," Toby rattled on. "You could have gotten some candy too." She cocked her little head, her curly blond hair bobbing. "But you can have some of mine, if you want."

Liza, who at fourteen thought she was above such nonsense as trick-or-treating, chewed on her lower lip. She wanted a piece of candy, and she was torn between keeping up her pout over their move or giving in to her sweet tooth. Garth bit back a smile as he watched her inner battle.

He could hear Carrie and Michelle in the living room, watching Saturday-morning cartoons and comparing their hauls. He doubted they'd share their loot as generously as their younger sister. He guessed the same thoughts were running through Liza's head, knowing that if she wanted some candy, she'd best get it while the getting was good.

"Thanks," Liza said grumpily. She snagged a piece of chocolate from the pile.

"We saw a lady come out of a coffin!" Toby told her.

The vision of startling blue eyes in a painted-pale face jolted into Garth's mind. He wondered what she looked like without the makeup. What color was her hair? What shade was her skin?

He coughed, suddenly feeling choked, and shoved away the questions in his head. At thirty-five, his love life was officially finished. The girls needed him, and they came first. It was just that simple.

"I was scared," Toby went on. "But Daddy held me. She wasn't really a dead lady, was she, Daddy?" She looked at Garth.

Carrie walked into the kitchen, Michelle trailing just behind. Like Liza and Toby, they, too, had the same gold hair of their mother and the dark eyes of their father.

They listened in on the conversation.

"No, sweetie, she was alive," he said. "I explained that to you. It was just a Halloween trick."

Liza looked interested, her dark eyes suddenly alert. "Neat." She turned and glanced at her father, all signs of pouting temporarily gone. "I wish I'd seen that."

"Toby cried, and Daddy got mad at the lady," Carrie said.

"He made us leave, and didn't even let her give us any candy. And she was giving away big chocolate bars!" Michelle added.

Liza's smile vanished. She cast a black look at her father. "It figures," she muttered, then stood up and stalked out, presumably to her room again. "He ruins everything," she grumbled from the stairs.

One step forward, two steps back, Garth thought. Just when Liza was opening up—boom, down went the shutters at the slightest provocation.

He decided the whole situation was just one more example of why he didn't need a woman in his life. That woman next door wasn't even there and she was causing problems. As if he didn't have enough problems already.

"Anybody up for some pancakes and bacon?" he suggested with forced cheer. He remembered he hadn't found the spatula yet, so he stood and went over to dig in one of the boxes again.

A chime rang through the house, distracting everyone's attention.

"Somebody's here, Daddy!" the three sisters announced.

Garth dropped his lollipop stick in the trash and made his way to the entry hall with Carrie,

Michelle, and Toby at his heels, all of them weaving their way around unpacked boxes and bags. Remembering only then to flip off the porch light he'd left on all night, Garth opened the door.

A tall woman with hair like spun honey and eyes like a cloudless summer sky faced him in the soft morning light. She wore a long-sleeved, pink cotton T-shirt and faded jeans that clung to her slender hips and thighs. She was unusually tanned for the first of November.

"Can I help you?" Garth asked, confused, wondering why anybody, especially this pretty angel, would be on his doorstep first thing in the morning. Her subtle cherry-blossom scent lingered around his senses.

"I hope you don't mind my stopping by," the woman said in a soft voice that teased at Garth's memory. "I thought I'd bring you these"—she held up a cookie tin decorated with brightly painted pumpkins—"as a peace offering."

She cast him a tremulous smile, looking as if she half expected him to slam the door in her face. Garth felt his stomach drop to the tile floor as he realized that it was *her*.

# TWO

"I hope this isn't a bad time." Kelly felt like dropping the cookie tin on the doorstep and making a run for it. She'd felt braver about the whole thing when she'd still been at home.

She was counting on not experiencing a repeat of the previous evening's heated confrontation. She merely wanted to repair the damage to neighborly relations.

Baking a fresh batch of Brian and Bethany's favorite chocolate-chip cookies and offering a truce had seemed the right thing to do. Surely anything had to be better than being on the outs with a close neighbor.

Unfortunately, when she'd come up with the plan first thing this morning, she'd temporarily forgotten how good-looking her new neighbor was and how he could have the oddest effect on her pulse. Particularly when he wasn't snarling.

Like now. At the moment, he was staring at her as if she were an alien. The youngest daughter Toby was hiding behind his legs, and the two other girls were watching with big eyes from the hall. They were all still in their nightgowns, while their father was dressed in a white T-shirt and jeans. He looked absolutely gorgeous.

Kelly focused on the children, trying to recall the names of the older girls. Carrie and Michelle. Yes. But which was which?

Anyway, whoever they were, they were managing to make her really nervous. Something about all those teddy bear–brown eyes locked on her at the same time. "I, um, I'm Kelly Thompson. From next door. You know, last night. I was the one in the coffin." The one with the fiasco, she bit back.

"I know who you are," the man said.

His incredibly dark eyes were a rich brown, different from the brown of his daughters' eyes. His were more like the color of whiskey. Intense and intoxicating. They shot a burn straight to her soul that was as unexplainable as it was undeniable.

"Oh. Well, I suppose we didn't get off to such a great start," she plunged onward nervously. "But we do live next door to each other, and I hope we can be friends. So I brought you these."

She stuck out the hand holding the cookie tin.

For a minute, she thought he might not take it. When his long fingers brushed hers and ripples of awareness shot up her arm, she practically dropped the tin into his hand.

"Okay, well . . ." She started to back away. She'd done her duty.

"Wait."

Kelly stopped.

"I'm glad you came over." Saying the words seemed to come hard for him, as if he knew he owed her an apology but wasn't eager to actually make it.

"I'm sorry about last night," he said quietly.

Kelly stared at him. She could have been knocked over by a feather. Just when she had him pegged as a brute—albeit a handsome, sexy brute—he had to go nice on her.

"We're all a bit exhausted and upset by the move," he continued. "I shouldn't have snapped at you."

"I understand," she said.

He looked relieved then, as if he hadn't been sure of her reaction, and he smiled. The warm crinkle around his eyes worked a contagious magic. She felt a rush of something sensual and shivery and smiled back. "I knew this house had been sold, but I've been out of town this week. I just got back last night. Where are you from?"

"Dallas."

"Oh." Hope was located about forty minutes north of Dallas. "I hope you like it here. It's nothing like the big city."

As much as Kelly looked forward to traveling, she knew she'd always come home to little Hope.

With the twins gone, it would be her home base instead of her cage.

"I'm counting on it being nothing like the city," he said. He didn't elaborate, leaving Kelly to wonder what he'd meant by the comment. "By the way," he went on, "my name is Garth Holloway. And this is Toby." He nodded down at the child hanging on to his leg. "And that's Michelle and Carrie." He gestured to the older girls.

"Are there cookies in there?" asked the girl he'd indicated as Carrie. She was the middle-size child. Seven or eight years old, Kelly guessed.

All three girls had bright blond hair, a contrast to their dark eyes. Kelly could see where they'd gotten their eyes from, and she supposed they must get their hair from their mother, since their father had a full head of short, thick brown waves.

*Mother.* Of course. The guy had to have a wife, right?

She felt stupid for getting all tingly from one little touch. The kids' mother was probably in the kitchen flipping flapjacks this very minute—and she probably wouldn't be very appreciative of Kelly having fleeting lascivious thoughts about her man.

And even if Garth Holloway had been single, it wasn't like Kelly was looking for a man, anyway. Especially not a man with a bevy of little kids.

Kelly focused on Carrie, deciding she had everything back in balance again. What a relief.

No more tingles, she told herself.

"Right. Cookies." She smiled at the child. "Chocolate chip."

"Oooh, I love chocolate chip!" Carrie exclaimed.

"Me too!" Michelle, the older girl, joined in.

"I love chocolate-chip cookies too," a tiny voice chimed in, peeking out from behind her dad.

Kelly bent down. "Hi," she said to Toby. The toddler studied her, holding tight to her father's leg. "I'm sorry I scared you last night."

Toby regarded her seriously. "I'm not scared anymore," she said softly.

"Good." Kelly grinned at her. The little girl grinned back.

Garth watched the exchange. Toby had always been his shy one, and he was especially protective of her. He was glad when Kelly stood back up, seeming to know instinctively not to push Toby any further.

"Thanks," he said.

She shrugged. "Well, I'd better—"

"Want some coffee?" Where had that come from? Garth berated himself. But he wasn't sorry he'd said it. For some reason he couldn't fathom, he just didn't want the woman to leave. Yet.

"I don't want to impose," she said hesitantly.

"You're not imposing," Garth assured her. She appeared to be considering his offer, as he watched her nibble at her lower lip. He practically needed a pickax to chip his gaze off the soft, delectable lip.

No doubt she was married. A woman who

looked like she did couldn't possibly have remained
unattached. She could tell him all about her husband over coffee. Hearing about her husband
would surely put a damper on the unwanted reaction brewing inside him every time he looked at
her.

"Well, all right," she decided.

"Great. Come on in." Garth gestured Kelly inside, and the girls scurried out of the way like mice.

Kelly picked her way around the unpacked
sacks and boxes, taking note of her surroundings as
she made her way toward the kitchen. She'd known
the elderly couple who'd previously lived in the
house fairly well, but the house looked different
now. Bare, she realized finally. No pictures on the
wall, no knick-knacks on the furniture. The living
room boasted the usual suspects—sofa, coffee table, television. But nothing homey. Nothing warm.
Just functional necessities.

She supposed the mysterious Mrs. Holloway
probably hadn't gotten around to pulling out the
family photos and mementoes yet. Apparently,
they hadn't gotten around to doing much at all.
Boxes were stacked practically everywhere she
looked.

The kitchen hadn't fared much better, for all its
sunny appeal with the big bay window behind the
dining nook and the apples-and-hearts wallpaper.
Unopened boxes lined one wall.

The place definitely lacked a feminine touch,
Kelly thought. Most women would have unpacked

their kitchen first, but it appeared to be last on the list there. There was nothing on the countertops at all except for a coffee maker and what appeared to be the remnants of the previous night's supper—two empty pizza boxes.

Weird. Very weird.

Garth set the cookie tin down on the kitchen table in the middle of a pile of lollipops and chocolate bars. He indicated one of the walnut-stained ladderback chairs.

"Have a seat." He nodded to Kelly.

The girls swarmed over the other chairs as Kelly sat down. They all stared at her silently. She felt like the object of a class science project.

Hadn't they ever seen a grown woman in their kitchen before? Of course they had, Kelly reminded herself. They had a mother around somewhere, didn't they?

Garth set to work making coffee.

"How old are you?" Kelly asked Carrie, hoping to break the ice.

"Seven. I'm in second grade."

"I'm ten and I'm in fifth grade." Michelle leaned her elbows on the table and rested her chin on her hands. "How old are you?"

"Michelle!" Garth chided, pulling his attention away from the coffeepot. "Sorry," he said to Kelly. "Don't answer that. I'm afraid they'll be checking your weight and height next if they're not stopped."

Not that Garth hadn't already estimated those

himself. Five-nine, he figured. A hundred and fifteen pounds, if that. Her waist was tiny, yet she was
curved in all the right places.

He swallowed hard. He was worse than the
kids.

"It's all right." She smiled. She had great
teeth—white and even. "I'm twenty-seven," she
told the girls without the slightest hint of the self-
consciousness many women showed when men-
tioning their age.

Julia, especially, had been really uptight about
it. Garth had never understood it, but he realized
now that he should have picked up on the signs,
should have seen what was coming.

But then he'd never imagined that the mother
of his four beautiful children would walk out one
day. She'd wanted something more and it was
pretty clear that Julia's idea of *more* had actually
meant *less*. Less of him and their children, that is.

"You and your wife must have your hands full
with these three," Kelly went on.

A familiar, clawing ache filled Garth's gut, followed by the shield of ice that made life bearable
whenever anyone asked him about the kids'
mother.

"My wife and I are divorced," he said quietly,
not expounding on the plain fact.

"Our mommy lives in California," Carrie
added.

Kelly's breath caught at the thread of pain in
Garth's voice. Sneaking a look at the kids, she saw

that Toby had stuck her thumb in her mouth. Carrie was chewing on her lip, and Michelle had sat back in her chair, her arms crossed tightly over her chest. The hurt in the room was palpable, if not visible.

"Oh." Kelly wasn't quite sure what to say. "I'm sorry to hear that."

"And there's four of us kids, not three," Michelle put in.

Kelly was silently grateful for the distraction. "Four?"

She swung a glance at Garth. Some woman had left him alone with *four* children?

His gaze remained level. "I have a fourteen-year-old daughter. Liza. She's upstairs." The coffee finished, he turned away and opened a nearly empty cabinet. He pulled out two mugs and filled them.

Four girls. And no mother. Kelly understood the bare walls and the pizza boxes now.

Remembering Garth's protectiveness, Toby's shyness, and Carrie's and Michelle's eager stares the previous night, Kelly realized this family was hurting—a family in trouble. She'd been there, with her own family.

Her heart ached to enfold the girls in a sympathetic hug while at the same time her survival instincts told her to run, not walk, away from the Holloways as fast as possible. And as far as Garth Holloway was concerned, she didn't want to listen to what her primal instincts were telling her about him.

He set a steaming mug of coffee in front of her, along with a spoon and a sugar bowl. "Thanks," she said, giving him a half smile as he sat down across from her with his own mug.

Sharing coffee with the man was hardly tantamount to getting entangled in his family life, she reminded herself. No need to panic.

"And you?" he asked suddenly. "You married?"

"No," she said. "My brother and sister used to live with me, but they're at Texas Tech now, so I'm by myself."

"Oh. I see." He looked almost startled by her answer. And then Carrie made her move on the cookie tin, jerking his attention away from Kelly.

"Hey, leave that alone! No cookies till after breakfast." Garth removed the pumpkin-decorated tin from the child's grasp.

The seven-year-old pouted. "But you let us have candy!" she argued. "Why can't we have cookies?"

Kelly spooned sugar into her mug, stifling a grin at the child's logic.

Garth seemed to catch the flicker of amusement she hadn't quite managed to hide. "I want you to know we don't always have candy for breakfast," he pointed out swiftly. "This was an exception."

"Yesterday we got doughnuts from the bakery," Michelle said.

"And two days this week we got to eat cold pizza," Carrie let on. "And another day we had cake and ice cream!"

"I want cake right now!" Toby joined in.

Kelly's grin escaped.

Garth looked embarrassed. "Really, we don't usually . . . We're not settled in here yet . . ."

"It's okay," Kelly said, glad the ice that had developed when she'd asked about the girls' mother had been broken. "I understand. Really."

"Thanks." Garth smiled. A genuine, sexy smile.

She felt another dizzying current of awareness. Her heartbeat throbbed in her ears. She had never been this affected by a man. Never. Where was all this heat coming from? Confused and worried, Kelly took a reckless gulp of hot coffee and burned her tongue.

"Oh!"

"Are you okay?" Garth asked quickly.

Red crept up into Kelly's face. "I'm fine." Her tongue was killing her.

"Daddy's a doctor," Carrie informed Kelly.

"Oh?"

"An *animal* doctor," Garth clarified. "I don't do people stuff." He looked mischievous, his eyes lighting with a surprising boyishness. "But if you ever need a rabies shot, let me know."

Kelly shook her head, laughing. "I'll do that."

A loud yipping started up from the back of the house.

"That's Beast," Carrie explained. "He's our new puppy. We picked him out at the animal shelter. He peed on the rug this morning and Daddy put him in the backyard."

"Oh." Kelly couldn't help grinning. She took another, more tentative sip from her mug.

"You're not a dog trainer, are you?" Garth asked.

"No, I work downtown at Holiday World Travel," she told him. "So if you ever need to make arrangements for a trip, I'd be glad to help."

"You mentioned you'd been out of town this week," he said.

"Mexico," Kelly told him. "One of the perks of the job is free airfare and other deals, like half-price hotel accommodations. Until the last couple of months, though, I couldn't take advantage of it very much."

Garth's brow knit with curiosity, and she continued. "Brian and Bethany—my brother and sister—became my responsibility when my parents died six years ago. Between school and all their summer activities, I've pretty much been glued to Hope. Not that I minded—I mean, I'm glad I could be there for them. I wouldn't change it for anything. But now that the twins are in college, I'm finally free to travel."

"So that's your dream then? Traveling?" His face changed, hardened back into somber lines.

Kelly nodded, bewildered by the abrupt change

in his demeanor, but went on. "That's right. I want to go everywhere." She took another sip of her coffee, about to expound on her planned weekend trip to Jamaica, two weeks away.

Before she could open her mouth, Garth spoke to the girls. "I want all three of you to go upstairs and get dressed right now. We need to do some serious grocery shopping."

"But, Daddy, what about breakfast?" Carrie whined, hands on hips.

"We'll pick something up at Burger Hut," Garth said. He pointed toward the stairs. The girls obediently slid off their chairs and scampered away.

The man might be remiss in the nutrition department, Kelly thought, but he certainly had the discipline thing down. His gaze turned to her.

Suddenly, she realized she was being dismissed.

"I guess I should go."

Standing, she wondered what she'd said to provoke the abrupt end of their conversation. Then she told herself not to worry about it. Garth Holloway wasn't her concern. And she certainly didn't *want* him to be her concern. She'd merely come over to make nice with her new neighbor, and since that had been accomplished, she should leave.

"Thanks for the cookies," he said. He smiled, but this time it didn't extend to his eyes. "It was nice meeting you."

He led Kelly to the door.

"Good-bye," he said.

"Good—"

He shut the door before she got out the second syllable, leaving Kelly on the stoop with her mouth hanging open.

# THREE

Three bright faces met Kelly's eyes when she responded to a knock at her front door on Monday afternoon. Carrie, Michelle, and a teenage girl. Liza, she guessed.

"Hi," three voices rang out in unison.

"Hi, girls," Kelly replied, somewhat surprised. After Garth's dismissal on Saturday morning, she hadn't expected to find any of the Holloways on her doorstep. Not so soon, anyway.

Kelly got off work at four o'clock, and she'd been home barely five minutes before the girls had marched over. The older girl held up the pumpkin-decorated cookie tin.

"Oh, you finished the cookies." Kelly pushed open the screen door and accepted the tin. "That was fast." She leaned against the doorjamb and smiled at the girls.

"We don't get homemade cookies very often," Michelle said.

"They were really good," Carrie added.

"Thanks." Kelly looked at the older girl. "You must be Liza."

She was a pretty girl, all arms and legs, just beginning to fill out in between. Just beginning to show the promise of beauty. Her dark eyes showed interest along with an awkward vulnerability that touched Kelly somewhere inside.

"Yeah, that's me," the girl said. "Umm, they told me about the coffin thing you did on Halloween. It sounded neat. I wish I'd seen it."

Carrie and Michelle nodded eagerly. "It was scary!" they both agreed, then looked at each other and giggled.

"Do you want to look at it? It's in the garage."

All three girls brightened. "Yes!" they cried.

Kelly motioned them inside and led the way through the kitchen to the garage. The girls took turns lying down inside the casket, then Kelly brought them back into the kitchen for sodas.

They sat at the kitchen table, holding tall glasses of soda and staring at Kelly.

"Do you have any more cookies?" Carrie asked.

"Carrie!" Liza scolded. She flushed. "I'm sorry," she said to Kelly.

"It's okay." Kelly grinned. "I don't have anymore, but we could make some, if you want." She wasn't used to having company since Brian and

Bethany left, and she realized with a start that she rather enjoyed having the girls in the house. She wasn't in a hurry for them to leave. "In fact, if you want, I'll teach you how to make them," she offered, recalling the comment that they didn't get homemade cookies often.

Liza bit her lip. "Really, would you? I want to learn how to cook, but my dad doesn't know how and he won't let me experiment by myself."

"He can't cook anything," Michelle agreed. She rolled her eyes.

"He tried to make eggs for breakfast this morning," Carrie explained. "He said we couldn't eat candy before school." Kelly grinned, remembering the list of breakfast foods she'd been regaled with at their house two days earlier. "He made scrambled eggs, then Toby spilled her apple juice on the floor and she started crying—"

"And Michelle found out Beast was eating her new notebook—" Liza put in.

"And Daddy got mad because Liza put red lipstick on," Michelle provided. "And Carrie said she wouldn't go to school until she found her new pink tennis shoes—"

"And Daddy helped me find them, but he burned the eggs," Carrie finished. "Then he threw Beast in the backyard and mopped the floor. And he made Liza take her lipstick off, and we went to the drugstore and got Michelle a new notebook. Then we had to pick up breakfast burritos at Taco Town and eat them on the way to school."

Kelly felt exhausted just from following that. Since most kids loved fast food, she got the idea that the Holloways must have been eating out an awful lot lately for them to sound as if they were tired of it.

Then Kelly imagined big, good-looking Garth Holloway bopping around his kitchen like a jumping bean, rushing from one domestic disaster to another. The image brought a smile to her face. And *tingles*.

He wasn't touching her or even looking at her. He wasn't even in the room. She was just thinking about him, and it was happening.

She had to stop thinking about him. Now.

"You're sure it's okay with your dad that you're over here?" Kelly inquired. She didn't want to get into any more trouble.

"I'm in charge till Dad gets home," Liza said. There was a touch of pride in her voice.

"Okay." Kelly went to work, surrounded by three eager helpers, preparing a batch of chocolate-chip cookies. She carefully let each girl take part, Carrie measuring the flour, Michelle stirring the dough, Liza setting the stove temperature and spooning the dough out onto the pan.

They sat down while the first batch baked.

"Will you teach me how to do my hair like that?" Liza asked, eyeing Kelly's French braid.

"Sure." Kelly motioned the girl to bring her chair around, then slowly went through the steps of creating the hairdo. After she fixed Liza's hair, she took out the cookies and put a new batch in the oven. Then they sat down with a warm plate of cookies and set to work again. "Practice doing it to Michelle," Kelly said. "And I'll do Carrie's hair."

The girls told Kelly all about their new schools, their teachers, and the kids in their classes. They were so busy chomping on cookies and talking about school and clothes and hairstyles that they barely noticed when someone started banging on the screen door.

"Who is it?" Kelly called out, both hands engaged in her task.

"Garth Holloway. I'm looking for the girls."

He didn't sound happy. Kelly glanced at the children. All three froze.

"Come on in!" Kelly called. "We're in the kitchen."

A second later, Garth filled the doorway between the kitchen and the living room. He held Toby in his arms.

He'd obviously just gotten off work. He wore casual slacks and a white shirt with a multicolored tie. He looked very sharp. Very sexy. Kelly's heart-rate took off at a frantic gallop.

"Hi," she greeted him with a trace of breath-lessness she couldn't quite control.

"Hello." Garth took in the scene—Kelly, her honey-brown hair sleekly whisked back into an intricate braid, his three daughters all adorned in matching hairstyles. The delicious aroma of home-baked goodies teased his nostrils.

The kitchen was warm and inviting, from the handstitched samplers on the wall to the lace-edged country-blue curtains at the window. Magnetized school photos on the refrigerator showed a set of twins at various ages. Flower-bordered recipe cards spilled out of a carved oak box on the countertop. The touch of a woman reigned everywhere, appealing and cozy. And feminine.

It was the opposite of the bare, underutilized Holloway kitchen. It didn't take a genius to figure out why his daughters had settled around Kelly's table like they'd found their long-lost homeland.

"Want a cookie?" Kelly offered Garth brightly.

"No, thank you." He could hear the tension in his own voice but could do little to control it. He turned to his daughters. "I want the three of you to go home," he ordered quietly. "Now."

"Daddy—" Carrie started.

"You heard me. Now."

Michelle opened her mouth, then shut it again. The three girls pushed back their chairs and stood.

Liza tilted her chin defiantly. The tautness of her lips projected a bitter, silent sulk.

Garth set Toby down and nudged her toward Liza. The little girl slipped her hand into her older sister's.

"I told you not to leave the house, Liza," Garth said.

Liza's pout grew more pronounced. "We didn't do anything wrong," she insisted. "We just came next door. You always ruin everything!"

"We'll talk about it at home." Garth gave her a long, hard look.

Liza stomped out with Toby, Carrie, and Michelle in tow.

"Liza hasn't adjusted to the move yet," Garth said into the thick silence that followed the girls' exit. He sighed, feeling overwhelmed suddenly.

Kelly stood. "It takes time to get used to a new place," she commented.

He shook his head. "It's not just getting used to a new place," he explained. "After my divorce, we had a housekeeper. She pretty much managed the house and the girls, their schedules—everything."

"She didn't come with you?"

"She didn't want to move to the country. And I figured I could handle it. Liza's getting older now, and I thought she was ready for more responsibility. Maybe I was wrong."

"I don't think so. She seems like a responsible girl."

"I have to count on her to supervise Carrie and Michelle until I get home," Garth went on. "It's for only two hours, and they're supposed to stay inside the house, with the doors locked."

"I think Liza takes the job of looking after her sisters seriously," Kelly said. "She just came over to bring the cookie tin back. And she was curious about the casket. It was my fault. I offered to make cookies with them . . ."

"She broke the most important rule on the first day." Garth dropped his arms from their crossed position and moved one hand to sift his fingers roughly through his hair. What was he doing? There he was, pouring out his troubles to a virtual stranger.

"If they come over again, I'd appreciate it if you would send them home immediately."

"Look, I know you're worried." Kelly walked with him to the door. "I get off at four every afternoon. I'll keep an eye on things, make sure they're not outside. I can even stop by and check in with them, if you'd like."

"No," he said, realizing immediately that his vehement rejection of her proposal sounded rude. "I mean, I don't want to trouble you."

"It wouldn't be any trouble."

He shook his head. "I shouldn't be dumping my troubles in your lap," he said firmly. "I'll go over the rules again with Liza."

"Well, okay." Kelly felt a little hurt, then silly. Why did she think Garth would need, or want, her help? Why should she even care?

Garth left. Kelly stared after him as he crossed the lawn between their houses with long strides.

"The cookies!" She ran back to the kitchen and opened the oven door.

Little black crisps met her eyes. Using oven mitts, she removed the pan and trashed the cookies. It was all for the best, she told herself. For the sake of her figure, she certainly didn't need to sit around alone pigging out on chocolate-chip cookies.

And for the sake of her heart, she didn't need to see any more of the gorgeous Garth Holloway.

"Start!"

The frustrated cry caught Garth's attention all the way across the yard, from Kelly Thompson's driveway to his porch. He leaned against the jamb of the open front door of his house and watched her.

She leaned down and pulled at the starter rope on a rusty lawn mower. The motor's weak cough carried on the light autumn breeze.

Kelly wore a faded pink sweatshirt and snug jeans; her hair was tied back in a loose ponytail that flapped back and forth as she pulled once more on the rope. Her small bottom was an appealing sight as she bent over.

Garth realized that he was staring and the sight was creating an uncomfortable response in his own suddenly tight jeans. He blinked and jerked his attention back to the house.

He'd spent the past three days, since their last encounter on Monday afternoon, doing his level best to avoid her completely. Unfortunately, the effort hadn't panned out. There she was, in full, feminine, sultry Technicolor.

He'd had no idea yardwork could look so . . . sensual.

"Girls! Come on!"

A thunder of footsteps sounded on the stairs.

Carrie, Michelle, and Toby clattered into the tiled front hall.

Liza appeared in another minute. "I don't want to get pizza," she groused.

Garth was simply relieved to see that she wasn't wearing that awful red lipstick. She kept putting it on and he kept making her take it off.

"We have to eat," Garth pointed out. He'd tried to cook the night before. An unmitigated disaster if he'd ever seen one. Even Beast had refused to eat the Mexican fiesta casserole he'd tried to make from a celebrity's recipe Liza had clipped out of the TV guide.

He wasn't up to another attempt. Yet.

Another coughing sound emerged from the driveway next door, followed by an annoyed "You stupid . . . *mower!*"

Garth couldn't help grinning. Didn't the woman know any *real* cuss words?

The kids spilled out onto the porch, and Garth shut the door. Kelly looked up. The girls waved energetically at her and she waved back, then shifted her hand to push back a lock of hair that had escaped its bounds.

She turned away, her shoulders slumping as she stared down at the mower. The shaggy grass in the yard around her house fluttered as the breeze rolled over it.

Garth gave in to the inevitable. She wasn't going to ask him for help and he couldn't for the life of him just get into his car and drive away as if she weren't having any trouble.

"Just a sec," he told the girls. He strode across the lawn to Kelly's driveway. He'd meant the girls to stay behind on the porch, but they followed him. "Can I help?" he asked when he reached Kelly. The girls hung back, watching.

Kelly whirled, her eyes alight with surprise. Even in her old clothes, she was stunning. Garth resisted the overwhelming urge to reach out and push back the recalcitrant strand of honey hair that kept rebelling from her ponytail. It looked soft, so incredibly soft.

And completely off-limits, he reminded himself sternly.

"It's this stupid mower," Kelly said, her liquid blue eyes meeting Garth's gaze. "It won't start. I've never tried it before. I thought it would be simple—it always looked simple when Brian did it."

"You've never mowed before?"

"No," she admitted. "My brother always did the yard. Since they left for college, he and Bethany were coming home about every other week during the first month or so, out of homesickness. But they've settled in now, and I've got to start doing the things that Brian used to do, like taking care of the yard, the car, and things around the house."

A ripple of edginess skittered up Kelly's spine. She should have asked Brian to show her how to handle all these seemingly simple chores.

"Maybe I should hire somebody to do it." Kelly sighed. The extra expense would really eat into her travel budget.

"Why don't you let me take a look?" Garth offered.

"I don't want to bother you." Kelly nodded toward the girls. They'd all changed from their school clothes into casual playwear.

Her pulse hammered. Garth wore jeans and a solid black sweatshirt—a sweatshirt that complemented his dark eyes and hair.

Kelly felt a shiver race through her, and she knew it wasn't the pleasant, still-warm Texas autumn air that caused it. It was Garth.

It was desire.

"Dinner can wait." He tucked his car keys into his front pocket.

"Aren't you on your way somewhere?" Kelly persisted.

"Just stupid Pizza Palazzo," Liza said.

"Again," Michelle chimed.

"I don't want pizza again, Daddy," Carrie whined.

Garth's mouth set into a grim line. "Fine. Burgers then."

"I don't want burgers either!" Liza and Michelle and Carrie managed to shout in unison.

"I want cake!" Toby said. She tugged at her father's jeans leg.

"We're definitely not having cake." Garth ruf-

fled his daughter's curls. She reached for his leg
and swung on it, gazing up at him.

"Please!" Toby pleaded, still swinging.

"You'd better get this crew fed," Kelly said. She
wondered how in the world Garth had gotten by so
far, with all these mouths to feed and apparently no
one capable of cooking. "I don't want to be a
bother . . ."

"No bother," Garth insisted. "Here, let me
take a look."

He unfastened Toby from his leg and stepped
up to the mower. His musky, manly scent pulled at
Kelly's senses and she struggled to push the awareness away.

Garth examined the mower. Then he glanced
up at Kelly, a mischievous smile percolating at the
corners of his mouth.

"What?" she demanded.

"Well," Garth said slowly, looking as if he were
trying not to laugh, "you do have to push down on
this little lever here to give it gas. You could have
pulled that rope all day and this thing wouldn't
have started."

Heat washed over Kelly's cheeks. "Oh."

Garth pushed the lever down and gave the rope
a good jerk. The mower started right up. "See?"

He tossed her a grin and Kelly responded in
kind, her embarrassment fading. The man was so
hard to resist when he smiled. It was a good thing
he didn't seem to do it very often.

"Thanks!" she yelled over the mower's roar.

Suddenly, the mower died.

"Oh, no." Kelly's face fell.

Garth peered into the gas tank. "You're nearly empty," he told her. "Do you have a gas can?"

Kelly frowned, then hurried into the open garage to search for the can. She rummaged around and found it.

"Dad, why don't you just let me go fix something for us to eat?" Liza asked her father. "I can do it."

"No." Garth shook his head. "I don't want you messing around in the kitchen without knowing what you're doing. You could very well end up starting a fire."

"But, Daddy, we don't want to go out," Carrie declared.

"We're tired of burgers and pizza." Michelle put her hands on her hips and gazed determinedly up at him.

"I'm holding you up," Kelly said as she walked up with the gas can.

"Kelly could teach me to cook," Liza pointed out hopefully.

Kelly blinked.

"Yeah, Kelly knows how to cook," Michelle agreed.

"Would you teach me to cook, Kelly?" Liza was fairly bursting with energy. "Please?"

Kelly's and Garth's gazes locked. There was no doubt about it, Garth realized. Since he'd decided against hiring another housekeeper, he could definitely use some help getting started on his own.

But could he let that help come in such a sexy package? The excited light in four sets of sweet-chocolate eyes held him back from shouting *no*. He wanted to find a way to heal his family. Home-cooked meals around the kitchen table didn't sound like such a bad way to jump-start the process.

If he was careful, made good decisions, he wouldn't have anything to worry about, right? Or was he such a coward that he was going to let his hormones stand in the way of what was best for his family?

"Maybe we could help each other here," he said slowly, still thinking.

"You're going to let Kelly teach me to cook?" Liza asked eagerly.

"No," he said firmly. "But maybe Kelly could give *me* a few pointers in the domestic department. We could make a deal." He liked the idea of a deal, a relationship of defined boundaries. An exchange of skills, nothing more, nothing less. He jerked his head toward his house. "I've got plenty of groceries in there. I just don't know what to do with them. You help me out and in return I'll help you take care of things around your house. Things your brother used to do for you."

Kelly listened. He was offering a fair bargain.

A dangerous bargain, considering the way her

nerve endings reacted every time the man's name even entered her thoughts.

She looked at the girls, then at Garth. Heaven knew, the man did need *somebody* to help him. And she could sure use the security of having someone to call on when things went wrong around the house or with her car.

Or when she couldn't figure out for the life of her how to start the dang mower.

She'd help Garth. He'd help her. No strings.

She could put a lid on the sexual attraction. Couldn't she?

She took a deep breath and let it out slowly, considering for one last second. Then she said, "Sounds like a deal to me."

# FOUR

"Okay, let's see what's in here." Kelly opened the pantry in the Holloways' kitchen and perused its contents. She could hear the mower buzzing outside. To speed things up for tonight, Garth had offered to go ahead and mow her yard while she fixed a meal.

Kelly was eager to take over her own yardwork—she didn't want to depend on her handsome neighbor for very long—but for tonight, with four hungry kids awaiting their supper, it seemed best to switch tasks.

"We have lots of stuff," Liza said.

"We all helped Daddy shop," Michelle said.

Kelly looked around. Michelle, Carrie, and Toby were standing in a semicircle behind Kelly and Liza. Kelly felt like the Pied Piper, the way the girls followed her every move.

"Great," she said to Michelle, then returned her attention to the contents of the pantry.

The shelves contained a strange collection of food—lots of crackers and canned pasta dinners, cookies and cereals with colorful cartoon characters on the boxes. Was this Garth's concept of having plenty of groceries?

Dinner was going to be a challenge.

"Baby food?" Kelly picked up a jar of fruit dessert with a cherublike baby sketched on the label.

"That's Liza's," Carrie piped up.

"No, it's not." Liza flushed.

"Is too!" Michelle insisted.

Liza's face stiffened. "It is not!" She cast a hard look at her sisters, then turned to Kelly. "I used to like to eat that stuff, like, for a treat, you know. But I don't anymore. I don't know why Dad is still buying it."

She lifted her chin. She looked so defensive, so achingly childlike and grown-up at the same time.

Kelly had the thought that Garth was having a hard time accepting that his little girl was growing up. She suspected that Liza was having a hard time, too, and she wondered how she could help.

She took a deep breath. She wasn't supposed to get involved in the Holloways' personal lives, she reminded herself. That wasn't part of the deal.

"I used to buy those baby cookies—the arrowroot ones—for my sister, Bethany, until she was in high school," Kelly told Liza. "She loved them." She placed the jar of baby food back on the shelf and moved on. "Aha!" She shoved aside two packages of chips and found several cans of pinto beans and stewed tomatoes. "I bet we can do something with this."

She moved to the refrigerator, her little flock close behind. Pulling open the door, she was happy to find a package of ground meat and an onion mixed among the sodas and luncheon meat.

"What are we making?" Liza asked.

"Chili." Kelly plopped the meat and the onion down on the counter by the sink. The window over the sink looked out on the Holloways' front yard and part of hers. She could see Garth down by the street, mowing in a straight line along the curb in front of her house. For November it was still warm and he'd taken off his sweatshirt at some point after she and the girls had gone inside.

Her gaze was riveted to his bare back as he pushed the mower across the grass. Broad shoulders glinted in the sunset, delineating each muscle in light and shadow. His strong back glowed with a sheen of perspiration. His build was brawny and powerful. Virile.

Kelly reminded herself to breathe and to stop staring. But she didn't, couldn't. She couldn't tear her eyes away from Garth.

Her examination moved to his trim waist. The man didn't possess an ounce of fat, which was surprising considering what she knew about his diet from an intimate knowledge of his pantry.

He must have good genes.

Great genes.

Incredibly fabulous genes.

Her gaze lowered. He wore snug jeans, which encased a well-shaped rear and long legs below. She wondered what his legs would look like in shorts. Maybe she shouldn't be in such a hurry to take over the mowing, after all. A flutter of heat spun up her spine.

"Can I, Kelly?"

Kelly blinked. "What?"

She forcibly jerked her attention from the scene outside the window, like pulling a magnet off metal, and looked at the girls blankly, not sure for a second which one had even spoken to her. She felt shaky all over. She was practically drooling. What on earth was the matter with her? If she was going to get this attraction under control, she was going to have to get a lot more serious about it than this.

She looked back out the window. Garth was gone, but she could still hear the mower, so she knew he'd moved on to another part of the yard. Thank goodness.

"I said, can I cut up the onion?" Michelle repeated.

Kelly focused. "I don't think so, honey. I think Liza had better do that part."

"I want to do something," Michelle persisted.

"What can I do?" Carrie piped in.

"I want to cook!" Toby cried.

"I'm going to help Kelly," Liza said. "You little

kids can go watch TV." She made a shooing motion toward the living room.

"No!" all three younger girls cried.

"Hold it!" Kelly broke in on the argument. "Everybody's going to help." Liza's lips settled in a pout. Kelly addressed the other girls. "Liza is the only one who can use the knife or turn on the stove, okay? You guys can help assemble ingredients and add things to the pot. We also need somebody to set the table. Carrie, do you know how to do that? For chili, all you need are soup spoons, bowls, and napkins. You can help by showing Toby, and the two of you can do it together."

Soon Kelly had each of them busy doing something. Carrie and Toby began sorting through the silverware. They piled the spoons on the table in a huge clatter while Michelle scoured the cabinets for chili powder and basil. The cabinets were a jumbled mess. The moving boxes were gone, but things appeared to have been put away without much organization.

Kelly leaned against the counter, watching Liza brown the beef and onions. "You're doing great," she said. She had a hunch Liza needed all the boosts to her confidence she could get.

The teenager shrugged. "It's no big deal," she said. "I can't believe my dad. He acts like I'm going to burn the house down or something if he lets me cook."

"Dads are just overprotective," Kelly put in. "It means he loves you."

"Was your dad overprotective?" Liza asked.

Kelly nodded. "I was, too, with my brother and sister, after my parents died and I was raising them. I understand how your dad feels. You're growing up, and that's as scary for parents as it is for kids."

Liza's forehead crinkled in thought as she refocused on the simmering beef mixture. "He doesn't have to be so strict," she said in a low voice. "Like how mad he got just because we went to your house the other day. He forces us to move out here, then he makes us stay in the house all the time. I hate this stupid town."

"I like it here," Michelle said. She produced a small canister of chili powder proudly. "Look, Kelly, I found it!"

"Great," Kelly said. She looked at the older girl again. She thought she could see a veneer of moisture in Liza's eyes. "Your dad just wants you to be safe," she said. "That's why he wants you to stay in the house. Pretty soon you'll make all sorts of new friends at school and things won't seem so bad here anymore."

Liza didn't say anything as Kelly took over and drained the extra grease from the browned meat mixture, then added the tomatoes and beans to the pot. Carrie climbed up on the counter to hunt for chili bowls while Kelly showed Michelle how to carefully measure the chili powder into the pot.

"It doesn't matter," Liza said suddenly. "I'm not going to be in this stupid town for long. My mom's going to be famous and I'm going to go live with her."

"Your mom's going to be famous?" Kelly repeated blankly.

"Mommy is an actress," Carrie informed her.

"She's going to be a star!" Michelle said.

Toby stuck her thumb in her mouth.

A *star?* That was interesting. Kelly opened her mouth to follow up, but Garth walked in.

"How's it going?" he asked. He had put his sweatshirt back on, and Kelly experienced an automatic pang of disappointment before she could remind herself that she was supposed to be glad he had himself covered up.

He smelled like grass and perspiration. Kelly knew she shouldn't find either of those things sexy, but on Garth she did. The man emitted some sort of animal allure. It was unnerving.

"Uh, everything's fine," Kelly said. "Dinner will be ready soon." She noticed Liza kept her back to her father, not looking at him, while the other girls all jumped up and ran to chatter to their father about what they were doing to help with dinner.

"I'm going to take a quick shower," Garth broke in finally. "I'll be right back."

He shot a glance at Liza and for just a second, Kelly thought she saw something haunted and painful in his eyes, then he left the room. She could hear him bounding up the stairs as she stared at the empty space he'd left. She thought about how much responsibility he was shouldering alone.

With just Brian and Bethany to raise by herself, it had been tough. Garth had four kids.

It's none of your business! she chastised herself. She shouldn't be longing for Garth, worrying about his girls, wondering about his ex-wife.

She concentrated on dinner, resisting the urge to ply the girls with questions about their mother. As the chili simmered, she had them preparing drinks for everyone and putting crackers on the table. By the time Garth walked back in, his short, thick hair slicked wetly to his head, she was ready to go.

He wore a fresh white T-shirt and shorts, and she tried really hard not to inspect his legs. She failed. They were powerful and muscular and sprinkled with dark hairs.

She looked up and realized he was watching her. "Dinner's ready," she said brightly. She thought she saw a glimmer of a smile at the corners of his mouth and she knew he knew she'd been looking at his legs. Heat flooded her face. She focused on the girls. "You guys did a great job."

She headed for the door.

"Where are you going?" Liza asked.

"Aren't you staying for dinner?" Michelle cried.

"We set you a place," Carrie said.

Kelly's gaze swerved to the table. She hadn't paid that much attention to Toby and Carrie's place setting.

"I don't think . . ."

Garth's gaze shifted from the girls to Kelly. "The kids really want you to stay."

"I should get home," she said.

Just then Toby came and wrapped her arms around Kelly's knees. "Don't go," she pleaded.


Dinner with the Holloways was an experience similar to being in the middle of storm—spoons busily clicking against bowls, girls all talking at once. Except for Liza. Garth's eldest daughter barely talked at all. Toby spilled her milk and started crying. Kelly was impressed by Garth's calm reaction. He simply got a dishrag and sopped up the spill, then poured Toby another glass.

The girls practically inhaled their chili, and when the meal was over, Garth instructed them to carry their dishes to the counter. "You can watch one hour of TV before bed," he told them.

Kelly wrapped up the crackers. She placed the package back in the box and returned it to the pantry.

"You don't have to help clean up," Garth said. "I'm sure you have better things to do."

Kelly shrugged. "It's all right. You bagged my grass, I'll help straighten up your kitchen. We have a deal, right? Fair is fair."

Garth leaned against the counter in front of the sink and regarded her. He cocked an eyebrow. "Ah, the fairness principle. I can see you've raised kids."

Kelly laughed. "Yes, with twins, everything has to be fair, fair, fair. Can't get one a new toy or an ice cream cone—or anything else—without making sure you've got the same thing for the other. It must be even tougher with four kids. How do you do it?"

Garth's expression sobered. "I suppose I don't. Life hasn't exactly been fair around here for a long time."

Kelly suspected Garth wasn't talking about ice cream cones or toys. He turned away, flipping on the water and filling the sink, seemingly uneager to pursue the subject.

"I'll dry," Kelly offered, taking up a dishtowel as Garth squirted some liquid dish soap in the sink.

"I'd use the dishwasher, but I forgot to buy the detergent for it," he said.

"You need to make shopping lists," Kelly pointed out. "That way you won't forget things. Speaking of shopping lists, I'll dig up some really simple recipes for you and bring them over tomorrow so you'll have them for the next time you go to the store."

"I could use a little organization around here, I'm sure," Garth commented. He turned off the water and reached for a glass.

"You got the boxes unpacked. That's progress." They worked quietly for a few minutes. It was an intimate, homey chore they shared. Kelly was surprised at how comfortable she was feeling with

Garth. "Why did you move here?" she asked casually. "I mean, why did you choose Hope?"

He dipped a bowl into the sudsy dishwater. "I wanted to start over someplace new," he said slowly, his gaze fixed on his task. "I had a friend from vet school who was working here, and I knew he was looking to bring another vet into his practice."

"The girls told me their mother is going to be a star. What's that about?" Kelly heard the words coming out of her mouth before she knew she was going to speak them. She sneaked a glance at Garth, hoping he wasn't going to clam up now that she'd brought up his ex-wife.

She was way too interested in hearing his answer to her question. "Interested" was an understatement, in fact. She was intrigued, fascinated, and utterly curious about Garth Holloway.

*And you know what happened to the cat,* she warned herself.

"Right. Julia wants to be a star."

Kelly couldn't miss the trace of bitterness in his voice. "You don't have to talk about this if you don't want to," she said quickly. "It's none of my business."

Garth shrugged. "I'm sure you must be wondering. Who wouldn't be? Four girls, no mother in sight."

He scrubbed another bowl. Kelly could see a muscle twitching in his neck.

"She always wanted to be an actress," he said.

"We met when we were both in school at College Station. She was majoring in theater arts and I was prevet."

"You got married in college?"

"Not because we planned it."

It took Kelly a few seconds for the impact of that statement to sink in. "Oh."

Garth explained in a matter-of-fact voice. "Julia quit school and we got married. We decided that it would be best for me to go ahead and get through vet school so that I could start making a living. Then I was going to put Julia through school."

"I see," Kelly said blandly, because she wasn't sure what else to say. She just wanted Garth to keep talking.

"I joined a practice in Dallas, but by then Julia seemed happy in her role as mother. She wanted to have more children. She really threw herself into the whole domestic scene—she was a volunteer at Liza's school, she was active in the community. She was always very busy."

"So what happened?"

"She got the kids involved in a children's theater," he said, "and through that she met some people who were involved with a local television production company."

"There are several TV shows shot in studios near Dallas, aren't there?" Kelly asked.

"Mmm-hmm. A few action shows, as well as children's shows. There are movies shot around there pretty regularly too. Julia started getting little parts in some of those TV shows, then she was offered a minor role in a movie, but she had to pass it up because she was pregnant with Toby."

Kelly digested the information, thinking she was starting to see the picture. Julia had married young, deferred her dreams.

"Where is Julia now?"

"Hollywood." Garth placed the last dish on the rack. Kelly picked it up and dried it as he continued speaking. "After Toby was born, she worked with another TV show that shoots in Dallas, and through that she met a producer who was impressed with her work. He promised her a part in another television show—out in California."

"What show?" Kelly asked, wondering if she'd unknowingly seen Garth's wife on one of her favorite programs.

"It was just a pilot," he said. "I don't think it ever got picked up. The thing was, after she went out to Hollywood to shoot it, she didn't want to come back. She liked it out there—it was exciting, glamorous."

"Were you planning to move out there?"

Garth drained the sink, his profile rigid. "When she went to do the pilot, I wasn't sure what was going to happen. If the show got picked up, I thought we'd probably end up moving, but I didn't give it a lot of thought at that point. It seemed unreal, I suppose. Everything was happening so fast. I just knew I had to support her in whatever she wanted to do. She'd been there for me when I was going through vet school, and I wanted to be there for her. What I didn't realize was that she didn't *want* me to be there for her."

"What do you mean?"

"I mean, I was in the way. So were the kids." He met Kelly's eyes then and she saw a bitterness there that belied his unemotional tone. "We didn't fit the image she wanted. She wanted to be youthful, free. Trust me, I've learned a person doesn't have to be middle-aged to have a midlife crisis."

"Is that what you think it was? A midlife crisis?"

Kelly would have used stronger words than that to describe his ex-wife's actions. She had to restrain herself forcibly from criticizing Julia's choices. It wasn't her place to judge his ex-wife, no matter how much she wanted to at that moment.

"I don't know," Garth admitted, his expression grim. "I know she had contacts, opportunities. Attention. Everything she'd once dreamed of. There was no way she was coming back to Texas, and she sure didn't want us to go out there."

"What about the girls?"

"I have full custody. She'd just gotten a small part in a movie at the time of our divorce and was about to go off on location somewhere. She agreed the girls were better off with me. When she first asked for the divorce, I was sick at the possibility of losing them, so I was relieved she wasn't fighting me for them. But at the same time I worry about them growing up without a mother."

"Liza thinks she's going to go live with Julia," Kelly said.

Garth's mouth tightened. "Julia has a regular visitation schedule, but so far the girls have been to see her only once. I don't think she really wants people out there to know she has kids. Children have a damaging effect on a youthful persona, you know. Especially teenage children. As much as Liza wants to live with her mother, I don't think it's going to happen."

He started putting the dishes away in the cabinet. Silence stretched between them. Kelly leaned against the counter, watching him. From the den the distant sound of canned sitcom laughter floated toward them.

"I'm sorry," she said, knowing the words were inadequate even as she spoke them.

Garth shut the cabinet.

"Nothing for you to be sorry about," he said. "It's not your fault."

"Raising kids alone is a tough job. I know. I've been there."

"We're making it." There was a touch of pride and determination in his voice. "We were seeing a family counselor in Dallas, to help the kids talk about their feelings. I haven't found someone here yet, but I guess I should."

Kelly suspected Garth was not a man who was comfortable with accepting help from anyone for anything. She wondered if he was already regretting being so open with her. He seemed to be dismissing her again, the way he had the first day she came to his house.

"I'd better get home," she said.

Garth walked her to the door. He reached around her in the narrow entry to take hold of the doorknob and brushed against her. Kelly turned and stared up at him in the darkness of the hall, which was lit only by the distant glow of a lamp in the den.

A crackle of awareness swept over her. The smell of liquid soap and chili and something else, something altogether male, filled her senses. Neither of them moved for a long moment. There was a look in Garth's eyes that mesmerized Kelly, a sort of aching, lonely hunger.

Then it was gone. Garth broke the eye contact and stepped back as he opened the door. "Thanks again for the dinner," he said.

"I'll drop off those recipes," Kelly said.

Had she imagined the hunger, the raw need, in Garth's eyes? For just a second she'd been almost certain that this man—this very handsome, sexy man—*wanted* her.

And the terrible thing was, she'd wanted him right back.

"Thank you, God, for Carrie and Michelle and Liza . . ."

Garth waited patiently beside Toby's bed while she repeated her evening prayer. His baby always seemed to take her own sweet time with the nightly ritual.

"And Daddy. And Mommy."

He felt a pinch in his gut, the way he always did when she mentioned her mother.

"And Kelly."

Garth froze. Kelly.

Toby—shy, quiet Toby—was warming up to their next-door neighbor in a big way. So were all the girls. Concern tensed Garth's muscles.

"And Beast. Amen."

"Good night, sillyhead," he said as he turned off the light, then tucked the blanket snugly around Toby's small body.

"I'm not a sillyhead. You're a sillyhead." Toby poked a chubby finger at him.

Garth planted a kiss on her nose. "Shh. Go to sleep."

The little girl closed one eye, squinting to keep the other one open.

"Close both eyes."

Toby squeezed both eyelids shut in mock sleep, then a giggle escaped.

"Go to sleep," Garth ordered gently.

He closed the door to Toby's room. His three-year-old was more right than she knew. He was a sillyhead, all right.

For a few minutes tonight he'd allowed Kelly Thompson to make him feel a little less alone.

# FIVE

"Hey! How's the old homestead?"

Kelly grinned at the sound of her brother's voice on the telephone. "Fine, fine. How's school?"

Brian rambled on for several minutes about campus life, girls, and professors. "Come on, admit it, you're lonely without Beth and me," he teased.

"Yeah, right," Kelly tossed back. "Okay, I have missed you. A little. Especially when I was trying to get the lawn mowed today."

"You mowed? No way."

"Well . . ." Kelly laughed. She told him about Garth. "But I'm going to do it next time, now that I see how to get it started. You could have shown me that little trick about giving it gas. I thought all I had to do was pull the rope."

Brian laughed. "So, tell me more about the neighbor."

Kelly sobered. Garth. Images leaped to mind of his sexy legs, powerful shoulders . . . wounded eyes.

"He's a single dad. He has four kids."

"Four kids!"

"They're all girls, very sweet."

"Do you like him?"

"Who?"

"The single dad!"

Kelly sighed. Brian and Bethany had gone through a phase where they'd worried about her love life. They'd even tried to fix her up with one of their high school teachers. She'd hoped they were over that stage.

"Good-bye, Brian," she said.

Brian laughed. "Okay, okay. I give up. Bye."

Kelly thought about the Holloways while she got ready for bed. She couldn't back out of the deal she'd made with Garth. She didn't even want to, really. She already cared about the girls too much to leave them in the lurch.

It was their sexy dad who was causing all the trouble. She'd just have to stay out of his way, that was all.

She reminded herself of that resolve on Friday afternoon after work. As soon as she got home, she went next door to drop off the promised recipes—before Garth got home.

"These are the recipes I promised your dad," she told Liza.

"Oh, can't you come in?" Liza asked, taking the envelope with the meal plans Kelly had copied from her cookbooks and recipe cards. "I was wondering if you would show me how to put on makeup the way you do. Whenever I try, I just end up looking stupid. You're so pretty."

"You're very pretty as you are, Liza," Kelly said. She took in the teen's eager face, then stole a glance at her watch. It was after four-thirty, and she knew Garth got home soon after five. She didn't have much time.

"Please," Liza begged.

"Okay." Kelly followed Liza upstairs to a big bathroom. Mermaids danced on the plastic shower curtain, lending a cheerful air. A small bench was tucked beneath the counter vanity. Liza closed the toilet and sat there while Kelly took the bench.

"I've got stuff in there." Liza pointed to a drawer in the cabinet below the counter.

"What are you guys doing?" Michelle asked, popping into the room. Carrie ambled in behind her.

"Putting on makeup," Liza said. "This isn't for little kids."

Carrie and Michelle gathered around Kelly, ignoring their older sister.

"We can watch," Carrie stated after a minute.

Kelly thoughtfully examined the array of cosmetic products in Liza's drawer. The girl had an assortment of bright lipsticks and colorful eye shadows. She had a hunch that what she needed to teach Liza was a little subtlety.

"Okay, first rule," she announced. "Less is more."

She went to work on Liza's face. Carrie and Michelle watched for a while, then started to play with the makeup, decorating each other's faces and laughing. Kelly meant to watch the time, but she was having so much fun that she forgot all about Garth until she heard him call from below.

"Girls! I'm home."

A pounding on the stairs was followed by Toby rushing in, her little curls bouncing around her flushed face. "Hi! Oh, pretty," she said, seeing her sisters. She reached for a lipstick. "I want to play."

"Liza?" Garth called from the hall. He stopped cold in the doorway of the bathroom.

Kelly watched him take in Liza's carefully made-up face, then Carrie's and Michelle's more clownish looks. She suddenly remembered what Michelle had told her days ago about her father getting mad at Liza for wearing lipstick. Judging from the scowl growing on his face, that issue hadn't been settled yet.

She felt as if she'd stepped into a minefield.

"Wash your face, Liza," Garth said tightly.

The teenager's features hardened into a rebellious glare. "Kelly was just showing me how to put on makeup. I wasn't going anywhere."

"I'm sorry—" Kelly started.

"Liza isn't allowed to wear makeup." Garth cut her off without looking at her. "Take it off, Liza. Carrie, Michelle, clean up." The two girls rushed to the sink. Toby slunk back against the wall.

Garth strode out.

Kelly rushed after him. She caught up with him at the bottom of the stairs.

"That was my fault, really," she said. "Don't be mad at the girls. Carrie and Michelle were just playing, and Liza was curious. She's fourteen. It's natural for her to—"

Garth whirled on her. "I know how old Liza is," he said, cutting her off. "I'll thank you not to tell me how to handle my girls."

Kelly blinked. "Well, maybe someone needs to tell you how to handle your girls if this is how you're going to do it. If you keep this up, Liza's just going to sneak around behind your back. Do you want that?"

She thought about Liza's collection of makeup. Obviously, the girl was already sneaking around behind her father's back.

"What I want is for you to stay out of it," Garth snapped.

Kelly glared at him. "You're right. This is none of my business. If you want to be a blind jerk, be a blind jerk."

She walked out.

Garth's anger deflated as soon as the door slammed behind Kelly. Seeing Liza wearing makeup after he'd told her not to had sparked his temper, all right, but he knew where his real frustration rested. It was with Kelly, seeing her there with his girls like that. Seeing them bonding. It scared him.

And that wasn't even the worst of it. Now he owed her another apology.

Kelly had just pushed the remote button to open her garage door on Monday afternoon when from the corner of her eye she saw the three older Holloway girls emerge from the house next door. They raced across the grass toward her driveway.

Stopping short of driving into the garage, Kelly lowered her window as the girls reached her car. The panicked looks on their faces alarmed her.

"Is something wrong?" she asked.

"It's Beast!" Liza announced.

"He's gonna die!" Michelle cried.

Tears streamed down Carrie's face.

"What happened?" Kelly turned off the engine and got out of the car quickly. "Where is he?" She walked quickly across the grass to the Holloway house, the girls falling in behind her.

"He's in the backyard," Liza said. "We don't know what's wrong with him. A little while ago I went out there and found him lying on the patio. He's breathing really weird and he can't get up!"

Kelly reached the gate that led to the Holloways' backyard and yanked it open, rushing onward. "Have you called your dad yet?" she asked, thinking that Garth was a vet and would know what was wrong with the dog. She didn't know the first thing about animals.

"No, we just found Beast a couple of minutes ago, then we heard you drive up," Liza said.

Beast lay in front of the sliding glass door that led into the Holloways' den. He was panting and looking generally pathetic, but Kelly wasn't sure she knew enough about dogs to say there was anything wrong with that.

"He can't stand up," Michelle said. "See?" She tried to lift the puppy onto his legs, but he collapsed with a little yelp.

Kelly's gaze zeroed in on the mutt's belly. It was strangely distended. Carefully, she reached down and tried to help the puppy stand, but he collapsed again, and his panting increased. A frisson of anxiety shivered up her spine.

The little dog whimpered.

"He's dying!" Michelle wailed.

Carrie started crying harder.

"He's not dying," Kelly said firmly.

"We have to get him to my dad," Liza said. "Will you take us?"

"Maybe we should call your dad first," Kelly countered.

Just the thought of seeing Garth again made her tense. She hadn't seen him since their argument several days earlier. She wasn't even sure what the status of their deal was anymore. She knew he felt she'd overstepped her bounds with him, with the girls.

During the weekend she'd tried to put him completely out of her mind. That would have been easier if he hadn't been out mowing his yard on Saturday and washing his car on Sunday. It seemed every time she looked out the window, she had to face some unclothed, muscular, *gorgeous* portion of his anatomy. She'd be glad when their Indian summer was over.

The man had a body like nobody's business. Especially hers.

"I'm scared Beast is going to die," Liza said. Emotion trembled through the teenager's voice.

Kelly considered her options. She really didn't want to be responsible for something terrible happening to the Holloways' puppy because she'd wasted time making phone calls.

Maybe they should take the puppy straight to the animal clinic. It was only a mile away.

"All right, I'll take Beast to your dad's office, but I think you guys should stay here," Kelly said. The last thing she wanted was to have another confrontation with Garth, and she wasn't at all sure how he'd feel about her taking his daughters out of the house.

"No!" they all cried at once, tears streaming from three pairs of eyes.

She stared at them. She knew how she'd feel if she was a child and this was her puppy. She'd want to be there.

She blew out a breath. "All right, come on."

# SIX

"Your dog's here."

Garth looked up from checking the stitches on a cat that had undergone spaying surgery earlier in the day. The feline's owner would be by soon to pick her up. He'd already seen his last appointment and was planning to do paperwork for the last hour of the day.

"What?" He stared at the receptionist.

"Your dog. Your daughters are here with your dog. They're all in tears."

Garth closed the metal cage that held the cat in the back of the veterinary office and made a beeline for the front of the building. What were the girls doing there? Moreover, how had they gotten there?

Beast lay in the middle of the floor in the reception area, the three girls hovering around him. But it was Kelly who grabbed his attention. She looked very businesslike in tailored beige pants with a simple white shell top. Their gazes met, and he could see the uncertainty in her eyes. The incident from the other day hung between them, almost palpably.

Garth felt an immediate wrench of regret that he hadn't already apologized to her. He'd had all weekend. He'd just kept putting it off. It was easier to resist her when she wasn't speaking to him.

"I don't know what's wrong with Beast," she explained, "but the girls were frantic. He's breathing hard and he can't stand up. And his stomach's swollen."

She knelt down by the girls to show him.

"Is he going to be okay, Daddy?" Michelle asked plaintively.

"Let's see." Garth knelt down and checked the dog. His stomach seemed bloated, all right. He tried to lift the dog, but Beast's legs wobbled and he collapsed. Garth frowned, possibilities clicking through his mind. "Come on." He picked Beast up and carried him back to an examining room. Kelly and the girls followed. "What has he eaten today?" he asked.

"Just his dog food," Liza said.

"You're sure?" Garth probed.

Michelle and Liza nodded. Carrie looked at her feet.

"Carrie?" Garth zeroed in on his seven-year-old.

She sniffled. He took her chin and drew her face up to meet his gaze.

"I gave him a bag of marshmallows," Carrie said, sobbing.

"The whole bag?" Garth asked her quietly.

"Yes." She burst into more tears. "Did I . . . did I kill him?"

Garth gave his daughter a stern look. "No, Carrie. But he's not going to feel very well tonight. It's not good for Beast to have marshmallows. Or cookies, or candy, or any other people food. Dogs eat dog food. Understand?"

Carrie nodded mutely, staring at her feet again.

"Okay." Garth gave Carrie's gold hair a ruffle. She looked up and sniffled. He patted her shoulder, then stole a glance at Kelly. He decided he wasn't going to put off their talk another minute. "I want you girls to take Beast out to the waiting room for a few minutes while I talk to Kelly, all right?"

The girls obeyed. Garth pushed on the examining-room door, leaving it ajar a few inches, and the sound of the girls' relieved chatter as they circled around Beast drifted into the room. Kelly stared at the door as if she'd lost a lifeline.

"I'm sorry," she said, and finally looked at him. "I should have called instead of hauling everyone over here." She crossed her arms. "The girls were really worried, and I hoped you wouldn't mind. If you feel I overstepped my bounds again by bringing them here—"

"No," Garth interrupted. "I don't mind. And you shouldn't apologize for anything. I'm the one who should apologize."

Kelly's eyes flashed surprise.

"For the other day," he clarified. He took a step toward her. Her cherry-blossom fragrance swirled around him. He stopped, marshaling his thoughts. "I was angry on Friday, and I took it out on you. That wasn't right."

She stared at him, her big sky-blue eyes still skittish.

"Maybe I'm a little overprotective sometimes," he added.

"Maybe," she murmured. Her eyes warmed then and the corners of her mouth lifted a little, and Garth laughed.

"Okay, maybe a lot overprotective." He kept his voice carefully modulated. He didn't want the girls to hear them talking. "Liza's fourteen. I know she's growing up. Maybe she's more ready for it than I am, I guess." He raked a frustrated hand through his hair.

"I don't think Liza's that ready either," Kelly said gently. "I just think she wants to experiment. I think it might be better to guide her than to restrict her so much."

Garth nodded. "You're right," he admitted. "I guess I feel pretty inadequate sometimes, dealing with a teenage daughter."

"I don't think there's anyone who doesn't feel inadequate when dealing with a teenager," Kelly said, trying to make light of the situation. "But there are some things that a girl wants to talk to a woman about. Like makeup, for example. Liza misses her mother. She's just hungering for a woman's touch, that's all."

*A woman's touch. He hungered for a woman's touch too.*

Garth felt a light sheen of perspiration pop out on his forehead. He remembered the night Kelly had cooked dinner for them and they'd washed dishes together. They'd talked and then he'd walked her to the door. He'd wanted to kiss her that night.

He hadn't really admitted it to himself before. *He'd wanted to kiss her.*

It was a total fantasy, and now it was loose, raging inside his mind, and it was all he could think of when he looked at her.

He straightened. This was crazy. "This isn't your concern. I feel like I keep unloading my problems on you, and that's not right."

"I'm unloading my problems on you too," Kelly reminded him. "We have a deal, remember?" She flashed him one of her heart-melting smiles. "Now, I'd better take the girls home so you can get back to work."

Garth nodded, relieved. Thank goodness. She was going to leave before he did something absolutely insane. Like kiss her.


Kelly spent the evening trying to tune in to her travel plans. She sat on her bed, comfortably clad in a T-shirt and sweatpants, the brochures she'd brought home from work spread out around her.

But she was having a hard time concentrating. The image of Garth—incredibly sexy even in his sterile white doctor's coat—kept dancing into her thoughts. He'd had to go and apologize to her, proving he wasn't really a jerk, and now she couldn't get him out of her mind.

She battled the distraction. She should be more excited about her trip to Jamaica this coming weekend.

Finally she blew out a frustrated breath and pushed the brochures into a pile. She *was* excited about Jamaica. She couldn't wait to go there, to go *everywhere*.

So what was her problem?

She frowned. Maybe it was just the constant *drip-drip* coming from the adjoining bathroom. The showerhead had been leaking for weeks, and it was worsening steadily.

She went into the bathroom and stared at the offending fixture. Hands braced on her hips, she glared into the shower stall. She had no idea what to do. She'd already tried tightening the showerhead, but that hadn't helped.

Her gaze swung to the telephone by her bed. Should she call Garth? It *was* his end of the bargain to come show her how to fix things around the house.

She waffled on the wisdom of inviting Garth into her bedroom but finally decided she was being silly. This whole sexual tension thing between them was probably all in her head. There certainly wasn't anything sexy about fixing a showerhead, so what was there to worry about?

Picking up the phone, she dialed the Holloways' number. "My showerhead is leaking," she told Garth a moment later. "Would you mind showing me how to fix it? The drip is driving me nuts."

"Sure. I'll be right over."

Garth knocked on the door a few minutes later. She opened it to find him standing there in a T-shirt and jeans.

He smiled and held up pliers. "Okay, nurse, show me the patient."

Kelly had an instant image of playing doctor with Garth and it had nothing to do with plumbing. A rebellious little tremor made its way through her body.

"Up here," she said, embarrassed at how breathless she sounded. She pivoted and headed for the stairs. She prayed this little job wouldn't take long because her body was having a hard time remembering that her attraction for Garth was supposedly all in her head.

Garth shut the door and followed Kelly. She was wearing a T-shirt and loose-fitting sweats, but that didn't keep him from noticing the sweet sway of her curvy hips swinging from side to side with each step she took. By the time they got to the top of the stairs, he was sure he was going to die.

He tried to focus on the reason he was there, which was not to admire her sexy bottom. "I'm glad you called," he said. "I feel like I haven't been doing enough on my end of this deal."

"I'm sure I'll find plenty of things for you to help me with," Kelly said without turning around.

Garth soon realized with despair that she was taking him into the master bedroom. Her bedroom. Garth took in the flower-patterned comforter with its matching pillows and bedskirt. The room looked like a garden bower.

"This is pretty," he commented, stopping and staring at the bed. This was where Kelly slept.

She turned, then flushed when Garth met her gaze. "In here," she said, and pivoted, heading for the attached bathroom.

Garth followed her. The house was nearly thirty years old, like most of the homes in the well-established neighborhood, and unlike those in newer homes, the bathrooms were small. Kelly's bathroom was no exception.

It was decorated in pink, and he felt very out of place. Cosmetics were scattered around the sink area. It was clearly a female domain.

Kelly stopped and turned, bumping into Garth. "Oh, I'm sorry." She jumped back a step.

Her feminine scent invaded him, intensified by the small space. He couldn't breathe without breathing in Kelly.

He realized she was pointing at the showerhead and he remembered why he was in the bathroom.

"Let's see," he said. He stepped past her, his shoulder rubbing against hers. He ignored the heated sensation that unwound inside him. He was going to concentrate on what he was there for and then get out. The showerhead wasn't leaking right then, but he could see the moisture around the rim. He'd turned off the water at the main valve outside before coming in.

He'd brought pliers and tape with him, and he set the tape down on the counter while he set to work inside the stall.

"These are channel lock pliers," he said, deciding to keep a running commentary going. Maybe it would help him focus.

Kelly peered in to watch him. Her honey hair swung forward over her shoulders, brushing his elbow as he went about his work. Her hair was soft, as he knew it would be. As he knew all of Kelly would be.

"I have all my dad's tools in the garage," Kelly said. "I bet I have some like that. What did you call it again?"

"Channel lock pliers," Garth repeated. She was watching his hands intently, completely engrossed in the home-repair project. Was she unaware of the chemical reaction that had him practically on fire?

He worked not to find this thought depressing. He should be glad that she didn't feel the same way.

"You take off the showerhead," he continued. Kelly stepped back so that he could move past her to set the fixture down on the counter and pick up the tape. "This is Teflon tape," he explained, keeping his voice brisk and businesslike. He quickly wrapped a strip around the exposed pipe, then took the showerhead and screwed it back on. "There you go. No more leak."

Kelly beamed. "Great! And that looked really easy. I can do that myself next time, now that I've seen you do it. Thank you."

Garth picked up his tape and pliers and Kelly led the way out of the bathroom. "I'll see myself out," he said. He didn't see any reason to put himself through another moment of torture.

"Oh. Okay. Bye." Kelly watched Garth hurry from the room. She sighed. Even though she knew her feelings for Garth were totally inappropriate, she had just enough of an ego to feel hurt that he didn't seem to be the least bit interested in her.

Of course, she was behaving completely irrationally. She knew it and she didn't care. Feeling cranky, she walked back into the bathroom and stared at the showerhead.

She fiddled with it, noticing that it wasn't dripping. She reached for the faucet handle to turn on the shower, curious to see if it wouldn't drip even when the water was flowing.

Nothing happened.

"What the—" Kelly pushed the faucet handle back and forth, from cold to hot, then to cold again, full force. No water came out.

She stepped inside the stall to get a closer look.

Before she could touch the faucet again, freezing-cold water suddenly gushed out.

Garth had just lifted his hand from the main water valve to Kelly's house when he heard a scream radiate from inside. He ran back around to the front of the house. He tested the front door. It was unlocked, and he bolted inside, following the sound upstairs, adrenaline coursing through him.

He raced into Kelly's bedroom, then to her bathroom and found her standing, soaked, fully clothed, in front of her shower. "Are you all right?" he asked, his heart pounding—first from the exercise, then from the realization that the T-shirt Kelly wore was very thin, very white, and that the bra that separated the shirt and her breasts was equally thin. The rosy points of her nipples stood out against the material. He had to jerk his eyes away from her chest.

He'd been so close, he thought. So, so close. One more minute and he'd have been back in his own house. Instead, there he was, back in Kelly's bathroom. And this time she was as good as naked underneath her wet clothes. He could see every line of her body and it was making him insane. He was worried that he'd already used up all his restraint while he was fixing her showerhead.

"I don't know!" Kelly gasped, swiping at water dripping from her hair onto her cheeks. She moved soggily out of the shower. "I was just testing the showerhead, but the water wouldn't come on, so I stepped in to check it out and all of a sudden water just poured out!"

Garth stared at her, grinned, then started laughing.

"I had the water turned off at the main valve," he said finally, trying to control himself because he could see the flames starting to shoot from her eyes. She was getting mad. "It's always a good idea to turn off the water before you start to work on a plumbing project. Did I forget to mention that?"

"Yes," Kelly said tightly.

"And I turned it back on just now, when I was leaving," Garth continued. "Then I heard you scream."

"Well, you'd scream, too, if cold water suddenly poured out all over you," she groused.

"I wouldn't be standing in the shower fully clothed with the faucet turned on," Garth teased her.

Kelly glared at him. She bit back the honest retort that it was all his fault—not because he hadn't told her about turning off the main water valve but because if she hadn't been so flustered from thinking about him, she probably wouldn't have done something so stupid to start with.

"Fine. Go ahead. Laugh at me."

"I'm not laughing at you, I'm laughing with you," Garth offered.

Kelly didn't buy that, but she wasn't arguing. She just wanted him to leave so that she could be alone with her humiliation. She crossed her arms over her sodden chest. She was cold, anyway. She needed to change clothes.

"You're freezing." Garth stepped toward her, concern replacing the laughter. "Here." He grabbed a towel and wrapped it around her shoulders, reaching over her. He rubbed her arms with the ends of the thick terry cloth.

"I'm fine," Kelly protested. Immediately she wasn't cold any longer. She was hot. Really hot. And it wasn't her wet clothes determining her body temperature now. It was Garth.

"No, you're not. You're freezing."

Garth kept rubbing her arms. Kelly's brain tried to tell her to escape from the erotic power of his touch while she still could, but the message couldn't make it through to her body.

His very nearness interfered with all normal neural functions. He was so close, right in front of her. She stared up at him. His velvet brown eyes seared her, and she realized suddenly, in some visceral way, that he wasn't immune to her after all.

He was just as aware of her as she was of him. The hunger she'd seen in his eyes before hadn't been her imagination.

His eyes were even more hungry now.

His hands on the towel stilled. Every nerve ending in her body tingled, and she could hardly hear anything over the pounding of her heart. She was only vaguely aware when he said something.

"What did you say?"

"I said, you should get changed. Your clothes."

"Oh." Kelly didn't move and neither did he. "You should leave," she pointed out.

"Oh," he said, but he didn't. He just stared at her.

Kelly's knees started shaking. She couldn't remember a time when any man had ever looked at her with that kind of intensity, that kind of longing. Her relationships with men had been few. She'd always been too busy with the twins, and with her own plans, to let herself get too deeply involved.

She'd never been tempted to get involved, to risk her heart. But the ache she felt for Garth was more than physical, she realized in a panicky rush.

The knowledge terrified her, and she knew she should move out of his arms before she got in any deeper.

Before she was lost.

Before he leaned closer an inch, then another inch, like he was doing right now.

Before he kissed her.

But she didn't.

# SEVEN

The kiss took Garth by surprise. He hadn't meant to do it. He'd just meant to wrap the towel around Kelly and go home. But he couldn't leave Kelly with just that one touch.

He wanted more.

Giving in completely, he deepened the kiss, sliding his arms around her, enclosing her shivering, slender body with his warmth. He reveled in the way she clung to him, her arms stealing around his neck. Her response was weak and fierce at the same time, and he realized she was enslaved by the same undeniable attraction that he was. She wasn't going to stop him, and at that moment he knew he couldn't stop himself. Nothing could have stopped him.

She felt incredible. Soft, warm, and perfect. Her body fit against his as if she'd been made for him and he for her. As if he'd been waiting, waiting just for her, all his life.

He moved his lips from her mouth, and she moaned softly as he slid his tongue along her neck. His hands progressed down her back, to her waist, her hips, her bottom. With her head flung back, she sighed, a whispery, *needy* sound that surprised him, nearly overwhelmed him.

Kissing her wasn't enough anymore. He wanted her body bare to his, her flesh against his flesh. Each touch, each kiss, each soft groan sent torrents of desire pounding through him. She tangled her fingers in his hair, pulling him closer, arching against him, welcoming him.

He was going to pick her up and place her gently on that big bed in her room, and then he was going to—

The phone rang and Kelly jerked away from his arms. Her huge eyes looked confused and frightened for a second, then she seemed to get ahold of herself. She ran to the phone in her room.

Garth watched her. His heart hammered madly in his chest. Regret at the interruption clawed at him. He felt breathless and shaken.

"Liza?"

Garth blinked. The girls. He'd left Liza in charge, and he'd completely forgotten about them.

"Yes, your dad's still here," Kelly said. She held out the phone to Garth. Her lips looked slightly swollen from their kisses, her cheeks flushed.

He crossed the room and took the receiver. Kelly moved quickly away from him.

"Toby's crying, Dad," Liza said. "She wants you to put her to bed, not me."

"I'll be home in a minute," Garth said. He hung up. He'd known it was almost Toby's bedtime. He'd known how she clung to their nightly routine. But kissing Kelly had made him forget everything.

His gaze locked on to a stack of papers by the bed. They were brochures. Travel brochures.

Coldness washed over him. What was he doing there? He didn't belong with Kelly. And she didn't belong with him. She wanted to roam the world, and he had four kids to raise.

He met her gaze across the room. She was standing there, in her soggy clothes, looking as nervous as he felt. He had an idea that she wasn't any more certain about what to say after a kiss like that than he was.

"Saved by the bell, right?" he joked awkwardly.

She gave a small laugh. "Right."

"I got a little carried away."

"Me too."

"I don't think we should—"

"Me either," she jumped in, not letting him finish, which was a good thing since he wasn't sure what he was going to say.

"I didn't mean to make a move on you," he said. He didn't mean to do much of anything he did around Kelly. Her effect on his equilibrium was disturbing, to say the least. "I feel like I should apologize."

"Please don't."

Garth nodded. He knew how she felt. He didn't want her to apologize either. They'd gone into that kiss together. They both knew it was a mistake. That was enough.

"This is embarrassing," he said.

"You could say that," she agreed, carefully avoiding eye contact.

He sprang into action. "I should go."

Kelly stared at Garth as he left. She felt positively limp from his kiss, and utterly relieved that he was gone and she could stop pretending that he hadn't blown her mind with just one kiss. She tore off her wet clothes, her body still shaking—not from the cold but from the desire that Garth had aroused in her.

Embarrassment flooded her as she remembered how she'd responded to him. He'd merely touched her, wrapping that towel around her, and she'd caught fire. It was as if she were lighter fluid and he were a match. One kiss and there had been a conflagration.

Staying away from him had been the right idea. She should have stuck with that.

She'd have to stick with that now. She was too humiliated. How could she even look him in the face after this?

She thought back. The kiss had been so overpowering, it was hard to remember who had even started it, but she was pretty sure it had been him.

He was interested in her, no matter how cool and collected he acted most of the time.

A little swirl of electricity unfurled inside her at that knowledge. She swore again, angry at herself, and pushed a breath out in irritation. There was no point in taking pleasure in the fact that Garth was attracted to her. No more than there was any point to trying to figure him out. And there was even less of a point in reliving the incident. It just got her all hot and bothered—and it wasn't all from embarrassment.

The whole thing had been insane, and she should thank her lucky stars the phone had rung, or she'd be making love with her neighbor this very minute.

And that would have been a mistake.

Kelly put on dry clothes and went to bed. She tried really hard to think about her upcoming trip to Jamaica that weekend, but when she woke up the next day, she was pretty sure she'd failed because she remembered her dreams.

They'd all been of Garth.

Kelly was laying out her clothes for her Jamaica trip on Friday afternoon when the phone rang.

"Hey!" she said brightly when she realized it was Bethany on the other end of the line.

"I'm coming home."

"What?"

"I'm coming home this weekend. I hate school. I hate it here. I hate everything."

Kelly frowned. "Is it school? Did something happen?" Bethany had always made good grades and she'd been excited about college.

"No, it's not school." Bethany started to sob. "It's Luke."

"Luke?" Kelly was stunned. Bethany and Luke had been dating since high school, and they got along beautifully. In fact, Kelly was pretty sure Bethany and Luke would get married, and she was just glad they were both finishing school first.

"He doesn't love me." Bethany sniffled. "I'm coming home. I just called to let you know I was going to be on the road."

Kelly bit back the urge to tell Bethany not to come. If Luke and Bethany were breaking up, this was going to be a huge heartache for her little sister. She couldn't walk away from her at a time like this.

She looked at her open suitcase, bikinis draped over the sides. So much for Jamaica. Her excitement about the coming weekend sank to ground level.

She'd been eager to get out of town. To get away from Garth.

She doubted she would have any trouble commiserating with Bethany this weekend over romance gone wrong. She sighed. "I'll see you in a few hours, Beth."

"Kelly said she was going to Jamaica this weekend. I wish I could go to Jamaica." Liza stared dreamily out the kitchen window. It was Saturday morning and the whole family was gathered around the breakfast table.

Garth tensed at Liza's comment. Of course Kelly would be going somewhere like Jamaica for the weekend. That's what independent single women did. That's not what parents of four kids did, and that's exactly why he'd walked away from Kelly's bedroom. From Kelly.

But apparently his mind hadn't caught up with his body, because it seemed to be there still. He couldn't stop thinking about her.

He realized Liza had asked him something. "What did you say?"

"I said, can I stay home this afternoon?" she repeated. "I don't want to go to the festival."

Garth had been planning to take them to Hope's all-day fair on the town square. It was a day of food, crafts, and games.

"No, we're going out together," he said. "As a family."

"I think it sounds like fun," Michelle put in.

Liza frowned. "I think it sounds stupid." Her attention arrowed back to Garth. "Why do I have to go?"

"Because we're a family, Liza. Families do things together."

"I want to do things with Mom," Liza said harshly. "I want to go live with Mom."

A spear of pain gouged into Garth's chest. He looked at the other girls and spoke in a carefully measured voice. "Michelle, Carrie, Toby, go upstairs and clean your rooms and get your laundry together. I need to speak with your sister alone."

The three younger girls scurried out of their seats and disappeared. Liza crossed her arms tightly and slouched down in her chair.

After a few seconds of silence, Garth spoke. "Liza, you're old enough to choose where you want to live. I want you to know that as much as I want you to live with me, I respect your feelings about this. But your mother is not in a position to take care of you right now."

"Oh, and like you *are*," Liza flung at him sarcastically.

Garth worked hard not to flinch. "I'm doing the best I can. That means I'm going to take all of you to the fall festival, as a family, because I think that's what a father should do. And you're going to come along, because you're my daughter. Now you're going to march upstairs and clean your room, just like your sisters." He kept his gaze level. "And after we clean up the house and get all the laundry done, we're going to go into town and have fun."

"You can't make me have fun." Tears glistened on Liza's lashes. "I'm *not* going to have fun." She stomped mutinously from the kitchen, pounded up the stairs, and slammed the door to her room.

Garth took a deep breath and exhaled slowly, his nerves throbbing, not sure whether to laugh or to punch the wall. He pressed his fingers to his temples and massaged the tension there.

Moving to Hope had made his relationship with Liza worse, not better. But they were there now. There was nothing to do but what he was already doing—keep on putting one foot in front of the other, believing he was going to find a way to put the broken pieces of his family back together.

"Who's that guy?"

Kelly came up behind Bethany at the kitchen window. Bethany pointed at Garth. He was standing in his driveway staring at the front page of his newspaper. He was wearing jeans and a sweatshirt, his bare feet exposed to the nippy morning air. His thick brown hair was still sleep-tousled. An image of Garth in bed passed through Kelly's mind, sending little tingles through her body.

She remembered to answer Bethany's question. "We've got new neighbors," she said in as flat a tone as possible. The last thing she wanted to do was display any interest whatsoever in Garth in front of her matchmaking sister.

"Really?" Bethany pivoted to cock her head at Kelly. "Does he come with a wife?"

"No, but he comes with four daughters," Kelly

tossed back. She walked away from the window and sat down again while she gave Bethany the *Reader's Digest* version of the Julia story.

"That's too bad." Bethany plopped back into her seat at the table. "He's cute." She cast a close look at her sister.

"He's okay," Kelly said casually.

"Oh, right, like you haven't noticed that he's a hunk," Bethany said. "Don't ever let me get as old as you then."

Kelly laughed. She was just glad to see Bethany lighten up this morning. They'd been up late into the night, talking about Luke. Kelly was sure that if her sister and her boyfriend would just talk, they could work out their problem.

Unlike her and Garth. There could be no working out of what stood between them, no matter how powerful their attraction. Kelly had given up her freedom once, when she'd become the twins' guardian. The last thing she wanted now was a whole new set of responsibilities that would tie her down again.

The phone rang. Kelly was relieved to drop the discussion about Garth.

"It's Luke," she whispered, her hand pressed over the receiver.

Bethany jumped up and ran to the phone. Kelly walked out to give her sister privacy. Several minutes later Bethany ran into the living room, where Kelly was lounging on the couch, drinking her coffee.

"He's sorry, he says he loves me, and he wants me to come back so we can talk!" Bethany exclaimed in a rush. "I have to get my things!" She flew up the stairs.

Garth was startled when the door to Kelly's house opened. Kelly emerged, with a younger woman who looked so much like her that he guessed she had to be her sister. The younger woman was carrying a small suitcase. Kelly walked her to her car, and within minutes the young woman drove away.

Kelly walked back up the drive, stopping in her tracks when her gaze met his. A jolt of pure sensual heat shot through his body from head to toe, and for a moment he forgot about all his problems. And he *wanted* to forget about his problems. Kelly made him feel like a man. Not a father with the weight of the world on his shoulders. A man, responding to a woman in the way men had responded to women from time immemorial.

Curling the paper in his hand into a tube, he crossed the lawn between the two driveways. He thought he detected a slight flush to her cheeks and knew instinctively that she was thinking about the same thing he was. She was thinking about their kiss.

He resisted the urge to inquire how her showerhead was doing. They were both better off pretending that the entire incident had never happened.

"I thought you were in Jamaica," he said instead. He was just being conversational, he told himself. Neighborly. Not that his thoughts were very neighborly. All he could think of when he looked at her in her T-shirt and sweatpants was what those same clothes had looked like when they were wet and clinging to her slender form.

"Yeah, I was supposed to go to Jamaica this weekend," Kelly said. "But Beth called last night. She was having a fight with her boyfriend and she wanted to come home and talk about it."

"Looks like things got patched up," Garth guessed.

Kelly nodded. "Yeah, her boyfriend called this morning and it looks like everything's going to be fine. That's why she raced out of here just now."

"That was really unselfish of you, changing your own plans."

"I love Beth and Brian. And I'm all they've got, you know."

"What happened to your parents?" Garth asked quietly, curious, thinking Kelly had done a lot of listening to him without saying much about herself. He was interested in her. *Too interested.*

"They died in a car crash," she said. Her voice was steady, but he could see the remnants of pain clouding her summer-sky eyes. "I was twenty-one, so the court allowed me to take custody of Brian and Beth."

"That was a lot of responsibility for someone that age."

"I knew that we had to stay together. It didn't matter that it was hard. It was important. But you know about that. You've got your girls to raise, and that's not easy, either."

Her words returned Garth to the scene in his kitchen a few moments earlier. "No," he agreed soberly. "It's not easy."

"Daddy!"

He rounded to see his four daughters, their sunshine hair brushing against their shoulders, pouring out of their house, crossing the lawn.

"Kelly! You're still here." Liza bounded up to Kelly's side. She was wearing a defiant air as she deliberately avoided her father's eyes.

"I had to change my plans," Kelly explained.

"Then you can come to the festival with us," Carrie said.

Garth stepped in quickly. "I'm sure Kelly has other things to do today." A few minutes of conversation with Kelly, that was one thing. But spending a large chunk of the day with her—that was something else altogether. Not a good idea.

Not when he had the memory of Kelly's wet T-shirt imprinted on his brain.

"Come with us, Kelly!" Michelle added her plea.

Liza didn't say anything, but he could tell from her expression that she wanted Kelly to come too.

They all did. They were falling for Kelly's sweet, warm, giving heart.

*It would be easy, too easy, for him to fall too.*

"Please," Toby begged, and put her chubby arms around Kelly's legs.

Kelly leaned down to pat the little girl on the back. She lifted her gaze to Garth. "Sure, I'll come. If it's okay with your daddy, that is."

"It's no Jamaica," he said quietly.

She straightened. "I know."

"Great," he said. He couldn't let his worries ruin the day for the kids. "Girls, are your rooms clean?" Their guilty faces told the tale. He shooed them toward the house and they dashed inside. "Is noon all right?" He raised an eyebrow at Kelly.

She nodded. "Noon." She headed toward her house.

Garth stared at her back, his gaze lingering on every delectable inch of her until she disappeared inside. It was patently obvious that he couldn't be around her and not want her, not remember with aching clarity what it had been like to hold her, not wonder what it would be like to kiss her again.

*And again.*

He had to think of a way out of this deal with Kelly. It was getting out of hand, and it had to stop. Before someone got hurt.

But first he had to get through today.

# EIGHT

Kelly changed her clothes three times, then had to ask herself what in the world she was doing. "This is not a date," she said aloud, enunciating each word for emphasis. This was not dinner and candlelight. It was a festival and four children.

So why were butterflies choreographing a dance number in her stomach?

Grabbing a cardigan off a hanger in her closet, she pulled it on over the dusty-rose-colored turtleneck she had combined with a pair of snug jeans and headed downstairs. Garth's dark green minivan was already backed out of his garage and warming up on the driveway. The girls were clambering into the back, leaving the front seat for Kelly. It was exactly noon.

"I guess I'm just in time," she said, her heart pumping a little faster when Garth turned to her and smiled. He was wearing a sweater and jeans too. He opened the front passenger-side door for her. "Thanks."

She climbed in. Garth got in and immediately began checking for fastened seat belts.

"Hi, girls," Kelly said. The three younger girls beamed back at her. Liza looked as if she wanted to smile but was trying really hard not to for some reason. Altogether there was so much energy in the vehicle, it was a wonder it actually needed gasoline to move. The kids were clearly excited that she was joining them for the outing, which made her feel flattered. And Garth—there was some sort of electric connection going on with him, and how she felt about that was better left unexplored.

"You're going to love the festival," she said, fixing her mind on something tangible and neutral. "My parents took us every year when we were kids." She watched Garth as he steered the minivan down the steet, his profile relaxed. It was a clear, cool day and orange-gold leaves swirled in the light breeze. Kelly felt her heart lift, her pulse race.

She felt extraordinarily alive. She looked forward to spending the day in Garth's company.

It was just a day. One day. So what if she enjoyed it? One day with Garth and his kids wouldn't bind her to them for life.

"I want to sign up for the three-legged race," Carrie announced.

"Can we go for a hayride, Daddy?" Michelle pleaded.

Kelly's lips tugged upward, remembering how Brian and Bethany had always loved the annual event. "The hayride is great." She twisted to face the girls in the back. "They take you for a ride out to the country in the back of these huge stakebed trailers hauled by horses."

"It could be cool," Liza allowed.

"You said it was stupid before," Carrie said.

Liza scowled. "Shut up."

"You shut up."

"All right. If you want to argue, we can go back and do homework and push-ups all day." Garth broke in to the rising heat of the girls' conversation with an authoritative tone.

The back went quiet.

"Push-ups?" Kelly inquired, sliding a look at Garth.

"It's the best punishment I've come up with so far." He pulled to a stop at an intersection. "They really hate them."

"I can tell." She smiled and met his gaze.

There was no sound in the minivan now but the hum of the engine. Garth held her gaze long past the comfort zone for eye contact. A jolt of electricity arced between them. The air positively crackled.

She saw the awareness in his eyes, too, and then he jerked his attention back to the road. The light turned green.

Kelly remembered there were children in the

minivan. She'd completely forgotten about them for a moment.

What was her problem? Wasn't the sexual peak for women supposed to be when they were thirty-five? She was only twenty-seven. There was simply no rational explanation for all this desire.

She was relieved to see that they were almost at the square. There should be plenty of activities going on at the festival to keep her mind off her hormones. As usual, the town square had been blocked off for the day, and as they approached the area, cars crowded—double-parked and catty-cornered—along the main road.

"Take that street," Kelly advised, guiding him with her past experience. Garth made a sharp turn onto a side street in a neighborhood of stately Victorian homes. "Now one more." She pointed to another turn and they found an empty street. "We'll have to walk two blocks, but it's probably the closest we can get."

"Everybody out," Garth announced after he turned off the ignition.

The girls climbed out, suddenly bubbling with chatter and energy again now that they'd been released from the van. Garth and Kelly followed several strides behind the kids as they all made their way along the sidewalk toward the square.

"Hurry up, Daddy," Toby called, then flipped back around, skipping to catch up to her sisters.

"I hope you're not going to be sorry you

came," Garth said. "This must seem like old hat to you. I hope you didn't feel like you had to come."

"Oh, no. My plans for this weekend were pretty much blown, so I don't mind." She didn't really want to examine too closely why she hadn't excused herself from the outing, from the opportunity to spend so much time with Garth. "The festival is always fun. It's one of the things I love about Hope."

"You've lived here all your life?"

"Every bit. I'd never live anywhere else."

"Really?" Garth looked at Kelly, puzzled. "I thought you longed for adventure, travel, exotic locales."

"I do. But I'll always come home to Hope," she said firmly. "This is my hometown. If I were to ever get married, have kids, I'd want to raise them here."

They reached the second block, nearing the square. Festival attendees flowed toward the center of town from all directions. She noticed that Garth picked up his stride to be closer to the girls.

"Do you want to get married and have kids?" he asked quietly.

Kelly pressed her lips together for a few seconds. "I don't know," she answered honestly as she kept pace with him. "I know what a big responsibility it is, because I've already been there with the twins. I never got the chance to be young and free, to sow wild oats. I was hardly more than a kid myself when I had to start being a parent to Brian and Beth. If I get married and have kids, it won't be for a while."

"After you've sown your oats?"

Kelly felt her cheeks flush, disarmed by the curious glance he gave her. "Yeah. That must sound silly, huh?"

They reached the square. The girls waited for them at the street corner.

Garth shook his head. "It's not silly. I'm asking some pretty personal questions, aren't I? You'll have to excuse me. I spend all week talking to animals, and when I go home, I'm surrounded by more animals. I mean, children." He winked at her. "In other words, I don't get much practice conversing with adult humans at all, much less with a beautiful woman."

It was all Kelly could do to remember to breathe as warmth unfurled in her stomach. He looked a little startled himself, as if he hadn't meant to say that. But he wasn't taking it back either. *Was he flirting with her?*

Worse, was she liking it?

And if yes and yes were the answers, what was she going to do about it?

Apparently nothing, she thought with a dash of panic as Garth casually slipped his hand beneath her arm. He guided her across the street, the girls fanning out beside them as they mingled with the crowd. Arts and crafts vendors were stationed on all four sides of the square, the majestic stone courthouse rising from amid the hubbub, its wrap-around parking lot temporarily turned into festival grounds. Among the paintings, jewelry, clothing, and crafts booths were food booths offering everything from buffalo burgers to tamales.

Strolling, they took in the sights and sounds and aromas for a few minutes. Garth put his arm lightly around Kelly's back. It was a casual gesture. Meaningless, she told herself. Nonetheless she was intensely aware of the brush of his fingers on her spine. Intensely aware of his maleness. A neon Danger Ahead sign flashed in her brain. And still she did nothing about it, didn't draw away from his touch.

They reached an open space, where a scarecrow contest was being held. A table was set up with ballots and a ballot box.

"Oh, Daddy, let's vote," Michelle cried, taking a handful of ballots and passing them out to her sisters, then to Garth and Kelly.

Glad for the distraction, Kelly dutifully took her ballot. She dug a couple of pens from her purse and shared them with the girls. Purposely, she walked in the opposite direction from Garth to start her examination of the scarecrows. Toby tagged along with her.

"You can help me choose," Kelly told the three-year-old. Toby's eyes were bright as she nodded with enthusiasm. Kelly took the girl's hand and they made serious business out of picking their favorite.

After they'd voted and stuffed their ballots in the box, they joined Garth and the older girls. Toby kept her hand tight in Kelly's, and Kelly was glad of it for two reasons. First, she was warmed to see Toby losing more and more of her shyness around her. And second, as long as she was holding Toby's hand, she couldn't forget she wasn't alone with Toby's handsome father.

They stopped at a handcrafted bead-jewelry booth. The girls huddled around a table laden with inexpensive necklaces. Liza picked up a purple-and-black-beaded design with a small silver heart attached and held it up against her shirt. Toby let go of Kelly's hand to squeeze between her sisters at the table.

Liza lifted her gaze to her father. "Can I get this, Dad?" she asked in a subdued voice.

"I said I'd buy you all something today," Garth said. "Are you sure you want to pick something out this early, before we've looked at everything?"

"Yes," Liza said. She chewed her lip, her face softening. Kelly had noticed a tinge of attitude between the teen and her father earlier, a hint of something going on beneath the surface, but it was gone now. "Please."

"Please!" Michelle chimed in. She had a necklace picked out, too, and so did Carrie and Toby.

"All right." Garth stepped up to the booth, where a jovial-looking middle-aged man sat with his arms propped on his belly, watching them. "How much?"

"You want one for your wife too?" the man asked, nodding at Kelly.

Garth's pulse picked up at the man's mistake. He glanced at Kelly. She looked uncomfortable. "I don't know, honey," he said, deciding to use humor to relieve the awkwardness. "Would you like one?" He almost burst out laughing at the shocked look on her face.

"Daddy!" Carrie squealed, her big brown eyes lighting up.

"They're not married," Michelle announced, then clapped her hand over her mouth, giggling.

Liza looked interested and Toby just looked confused.

How would the girls feel if he ever did start dating? Garth wondered suddenly. He hadn't given it much thought up to this point. He hadn't ever planned to date. But was that a realistic decision?

It was Kelly who had him thinking about it. She had him thinking about a lot of things.

She had him doing things too. Flirting with her. Touching her. *Kissing her*. Things he shouldn't be doing.

"Four necklaces," Garth said to the man after Kelly declined to take one. "How much?" He pulled out his wallet, his genial mood dampened. If he started dating, it wouldn't be with his sexy neighbor. She was going to be busy sowing wild oats, and he wasn't dumb enough to think a guy with four kids could possibly be anybody's idea of *that*.

He handed the money across the table while Kelly helped the younger girls fasten their necklaces around their necks.

They found the outdoor stage next. A puppet show was about to start.

"This is totally lame." Liza was scornful, her arms crossed in a belligerent pose. The glow from the necklace purchase seemed to have worn off already. She fingered the silver heart, looking bored and irritable. Garth was positive the only reason she'd kept her bad attitude in check thus far was because Kelly had come along.

"Hey, Liza!" A pretty red-haired girl who looked to be about Liza's age approached the group. He was surprised to see his daughter smile.

Liza hung back to speak with her friend while Garth settled the other girls into front-row seats. By the time he returned to where Kelly was standing, Liza was back, the girl with the red hair at her side.

"Can I walk around with Tammy for a while, Dad?"

Garth responded to the excitement on his daughter's face. He missed the happy girl she'd once been before she'd been replaced by a moody, scowling teenager. Maybe if she developed some real friendships, she'd be happier in Hope. Happier in general.

He checked his watch. "I want you to meet us at the entrance to the park off of the town square at five o'clock," he said. "And remember, don't have fun," he couldn't resist adding teasingly.

Liza's lips tightened and she rolled her eyes expressively at her friend. The two girls headed off into the crowd.

Garth sighed.

"Fourteen is a painful age," Kelly commented.

Garth met her eyes for the first time since the jewelry-booth incident. "For parents or for kids?"

"Both."

"What about fifteen?"

"It's painful too."

"Sixteen?"

"They start driving."

He groaned. "You're scaring me. Come on, let's sit down."

They grabbed a spot in the back, where they wouldn't block the view for any children. The seats were on long wooden benches, and as kids filled up the benches in front of them, parents squeezed in beside them until Garth found his thigh and shoulder brushing Kelly's. Festivalgoers milled past the perimeter of the makeshift outdoor theater.

Kelly faced forward, appearing to concentrate on the stage. Garth tried, but the kids' show couldn't compete with the impossibly gorgeous woman whose leg and side were pressed against him.

Visions of the last time he'd gotten this close to Kelly danced in his head: her skin seductive and soft, her mouth hot and hungry. The intense desire to repeat that moment zinged through him. The temperature was no more than sixty-five degrees, but he was burning up inside.

"About Liza," Kelly was saying. "I didn't really mean to scare you. The teen years aren't all bad."

Garth gave a huff of laughter. "That's a relief." He paused. "We had a run-in this morning over coming to the festival. All she ever wants to do is sit in her room and brood."

"Teenagers are pretty brooding," Kelly said. "I don't think that's too unusual." She gave the situation some thought. "What does Liza like to do? Is there some interest the two of you have in common? I collected stamps when I was a kid, and that was something my dad and I did together—poring over catalogs and searching out special stamps in collector shops."

"Is that how you got interested in travel?"

"My parents always talked about traveling." Kelly tilted her head back in thought. "Their favorite topic of conversation was all the places they were going to go to when they retired." Her expression grew solemn. "That never happened."

"Didn't you go on trips as a family?" Garth asked.

"We never had the money," she said. "Or the time. There were all those sports and dance recitals and school activities. There was always something standing in the way. The farthest we ever went when I was a kid was a trip to Oklahoma, where my grandparents lived, but I dreamed of going to all those places my parents were always talking about."

"Where?"

"Europe," Kelly said immediately. "Paris, London, Rome, Vienna—everywhere. I want to see castles and great rivers and monuments and museums, and, oh, just everything. I've got to really save up for those kinds of trips, though. The trips I've got planned right now—Caribbean resorts and this cruise I'm taking at Christmas—aren't as expensive as they sound. I get a lot of special deals as a travel agent."

"And this, of course, is why you became a travel agent."

"The perks are great."

She smiled.

Garth found himself watching her mouth, thinking what those lips had felt like crushed beneath his. He jerked himself back to reality, where her lips and his weren't destined to meet again.

"My dad had one of those big globes that fit into a stand, the kind you can spin around." She took a deep breath, exhaling slowly, her gaze moving over the crowd of children in front of them as she went on. "I used to spin it, close my eyes, and stop it with my finger. Wherever it stopped, I would run to the encyclopedia and look the place up so that I could pretend I was going to go there someday. I made this huge list of places I wanted to go—places my parents talked about, places I found on the globe myself." A flush stained her cheeks as she met his eyes. "I was a weird kid."

Garth shook his head. "You were a dreamer."

"Most people are. Dreamers, I mean. I bet you always wanted to be a vet."

He remembered the way he'd tormented the neighborhood pets in his endless attempts to poke, prod, and bandage their healthy bodies. The conversation made him think about Julia and how her dreams had shattered their family. He hated the bitterness that thought brought with it. "Dreams are powerful," he said grimly, looking away.

They watched the puppet show quietly for a few minutes.

"How are you doing in the cooking department?" Kelly asked.

He shifted his gaze back to her. "I burned your spaghetti pie recipe when Toby overflowed the bathtub on Tuesday," he told her. "So I tried it again on Wednesday."

"And?"

"It was good. The girls loved it. They liked it on Thursday too. But they were tired of it by Friday."

"You made spaghetti pie every day this week?"

Garth smiled slightly. "I tripled the batch on Wednesday so that it would last. I thought that way I wouldn't have to come home every night and cook. I thought this was a great idea. Unfortunately, I was the only one who did."

Kelly laughed. "Mmm. I can see why."

She recrossed her legs, shifting her balance, and Garth noticed afresh the warmth of her leg against his own.

"What are your other interests?" she asked. "Besides learning to cook . . ."

She watched him with her guileless blue eyes, seemingly unaware of the chaos her closeness was inciting. What were his interests, his needs? Those weren't things he gave much thought to anymore—what he enjoyed, what he wanted.

*He wanted Kelly.* Despite the fact that she'd just recited all the reasons he shouldn't want her—her dreams—he wanted her just the same.

"Camping," he answered, battling for focus. "I was an Eagle Scout, and I always loved hiking and exploring. I don't have time for any of that now, though. The girls certainly aren't interested in the outdoors."

"Are you sure? Maybe you should take them camping."

Garth's brows shot up. "Liza? Camping? What would she do without mirrors and hair spray and stereo speakers?" he asked dryly.

Kelly gave him a serious look. "Maybe you should find out," she said. "There's not much else to do in the middle of the woods but talk, you know."

"You've got a point." Applause broke out around them and he realized the puppet show was over.

They gathered the kids and explored another street of booths before making their way toward the park just off the square. Carrie and Michelle participated in some of the kids' games and won several second- and third-place ribbons each.

"The grown-ups are going to do the three-legged race now," Michelle said when she ran up at the end of a game, face flushed, ribbons proudly clutched in her hand. "You and Kelly could play," she suggested.

Kelly's gaze flashed to Garth. "I don't know . . ." she started.

"Chicken?" He couldn't resist teasing her. He was enjoying today, and he wasn't going to think about tomorrow. Not yet, at least. Not as long as it was still daylight. "Afraid you can't keep up with me?" The idea of getting into a potato sack with Kelly was incredibly appealing.

"I was on the track team in high school, I'll have you know," Kelly said, lifting her chin and taking up his challenge.

"All right then. It's settled. Let's show these girls how to win first place," he said.

He took her arm. She still looked reluctant, but her eyes were bright, excited, and he knew she felt what he felt—the odd spark of something unknown and powerful. Something between them. It couldn't be—whatever it was—and somehow that seemed to make it even more intense.

They were playing with fire.

About a dozen pairs were being herded toward the starting line. Garth and Kelly picked up their own big burlap sack and found a place at one end. The three girls sat at the side of the marked-off competition area to watch.

Garth stuck his foot in the sack. "Okay." He held it open and looked at Kelly.

She slid her foot inside, seeming to hold her body carefully away from Garth. "Which feet are we going to start with?" she asked.

"Let's start together, with the inside feet," Garth decided.

The announcer started the countdown.

Garth slipped his arm around Kelly's waist. She looked up at him, startled. He hugged her closer. "Teamwork," he said.

"Three—go!"

They were off. Couples raced forward. Kelly was still staring at Garth and started off on the wrong foot. He pulled her along, his arm behind her back, but they were halfway up the field, behind everyone, before they got synchronized. They started to catch up, passed two couples who'd fallen, then Garth tripped.

He knew he was going down, and he had just enough time to tug Kelly around so that she fell on top of him rather than beside him.

She landed on him with a small scream and he grabbed her tight. Her body felt light and soft.

"I'm sorry," she said as soon as she could, the

words coming out between gasps for air. "Was that my fault?" She stared down at him, the cloudless blue sky framing her.

"I think it was my fault." Garth didn't move, just held her, didn't want to let go. His ankle ached, so he knew he'd twisted it a little, but he didn't care about that.

"I should get off you. I must be killing you."

Garth smiled. "Hmm. I kind of like this position. Don't move." He wondered if he'd knocked his head in the fall. He was saying exactly what he was thinking, without censoring himself. The people around them receded, until there was just soft grass beneath them, blue sky above them, and their hearts pumping hard and fast, their bodies molded against each other's. "This feels good." He slid his hand behind her neck, drew her closer. "Don't you think?"

She said, "Yes," without a second's hesitation, then her eyes widened as if she'd just realized what she'd done. Her next words came out breathlessly fast, nervous, and close. "Garth, there are about a hundred people watching us. We can't—"

"Can't what?" Was she thinking about kissing him? He knew that he was. He could raise up just so and—

She wriggled out of his arms and rolled off. "We lost," she said instead, hastily changing the subject and avoiding his eyes.

"Apparently," he said, suddenly feeling flat.

Kelly was gone, and with her went the magic. It had to be a spell—what else could explain how all he had to do was touch her and every ounce of self-restraint and good sense seemed to vanish? He'd almost kissed her. He'd wanted to kiss her. He hadn't cared how many people were watching.

He noticed that they were the only ones left on the field. Even the other fallen couples had gotten up and finished the race. The ribbons were being handed out. The onlookers were dispersing. Carrie, Michelle, and Toby started to run across the grass to them.

"We got off to a bad start. That was my fault." Kelly sat up, peeling back the sack. "Are you all right?" She stared hard at his foot, but her cheeks were red, and he wondered if it was just the nippy air and physical exertion that were responsible for her color.

"I'm fine." He got up, tested his ankle. She stood, watching him. "See, it's fine."

The girls reached them, and that was it. They went on their way. The park was filled with crafts-people. There was a man with an old mill grinding corn into meal, and there were potters and leather workers and blacksmiths. Toby had daisies painted on her cheeks at a face-painting booth. And the moment when Garth might have kissed Kelly again was as if it had never been. Except that every time his eyes met hers, he wondered if she'd been thinking the same thing he had.

If she'd wanted the same thing he had.

At five o'clock, they headed back to the park entrance and found Liza waiting obediently on a bench. The weather was perfect—brisk but not too cold. They found a spot of soft grass under a tree and ate corn dogs and drank lemonade out of huge plastic cups. Eventually even Liza relaxed, sprawling out on the ground with her sisters and forgetting to wear her attitude.

Garth thought about the jewelry vendor who'd mistaken Kelly for his wife. Indeed, he knew they must look like a family to any outsider. A perfect family.

The idea of Kelly as part of his family, by his side forever, was tantalizing. It was a fantasy and he knew it, but he indulged in it, anyway. Just for a few minutes.

Afterward, they took in several street performances by high school students and senior citizen groups. The hayride was last, at dusk. The hay was sweet-smelling and fresh, soft and prickly all at once. The trailers, which had been embarking on a ride on the hour every hour throughout the day, were still packing in the people. The trailer Garth, Kelly, and the kids climbed onto was no different. Garth took Toby on his lap. The other three girls cuddled up to one side of him, leaving Kelly to settle in on the other. She made a nest for herself in the hay, allowing several inches of careful distance between them.

The horses clip-clopped through town and onto a country road while the laughter and chatter of his children rained down around them. Garth leaned back and looked up at the sky, at the pink and gold streaks left behind by the setting sun. The rhythmic sway of the rig jostled Kelly against him. It was oddly comfortable and yet exciting at the same time. He enjoyed the way the dying light shimmered in her dark hair, the way she smiled at his children, the way her eyes lit with awareness whenever her gaze slid to his.

He couldn't help thinking about what it would be like to be alone in that deep pile of sweet hay with Kelly.

Darkness had seized the remnants of the day by the time they returned to the square. The walk to the minivan seemed longer than it had earlier in the day. When they pulled into their garage, the girls were drooping with exhaustion. They stumbled into the house.

"Brush your teeth and get ready for bed," Garth called. He followed Kelly out to the driveway, reluctant for their day together to end and knowing at the same time that it *had* to end. That there were too many things that stood between them. That there was no room in his life for a fantasy.

So why was it so hard to let go of the fantasy? He prayed he would find the strength.

"Kelly."

She turned at the rough, gentle sound of

Garth's voice. The light spilling from the garage framed him, leaving his face shadowed by the night.

"Thanks for today," he said. "You forgot to leave your porch light on. I'll walk you home."

"You don't have to. We don't have bad guys in the bushes in Hope. It's not the big city."

"You can't be too careful," he said. "I wouldn't feel right if I didn't walk you home."

"Well, all right then."

It occurred to Kelly that it wasn't being very careful to take a walk in the dark with Garth, but she fell into step with him without further argument anyway. She was extremely aware of him as they crossed the yard. He was within touching range—yet she couldn't touch him. Which only made her want to touch him more.

The distance between the two houses wasn't great, to both her relief and her regret. "I enjoyed today," she said as they reached her porch. She scrounged through her purse, finding her key by touch. "Thank you for inviting me."

"You're good with the girls," Garth said. "They like you a lot, you know."

"I like them too. They're sweet. Even Liza."

Garth made a doubtful sound.

"She is," Kelly insisted.

He watched her, his gaze steady in the darkness. "I keep thinking about what you said about camping. It was a good idea. Thank you."

"You're welcome."

Leaves rustled in the trees as the breeze picked up for a few seconds, then died down again. The air was nippy now that the sun had gone down. She was shivering a little, but she wasn't sure if it was the temperature outside or the proximity of Garth that caused it.

"I'm home," she pointed out.

Garth looked down at her, his features illuminated by the distant streetlight. Their gazes met and Kelly knew he was going to kiss her, really kiss her, this time. Not just think about it.

She didn't resist, didn't waste time on second thoughts. He pulled her close. His body molded against hers felt sinfully good—all broad shoulders and hard muscles. She wasn't cold anymore. Her arms crept about his neck as she melted into his kiss, opening her mouth eagerly to his plunder. He tasted like sunshine and lemonade and man, and he wanted her. The knowledge was heady.

He buried his fingers in her hair as he deepened the kiss. The proof of his arousal pressed hotly against her. Then he drew back suddenly, gasping for air.

"Kelly," he said raggedly, releasing her. She almost stumbled at the abrupt loss of his supporting arms. "I can't say this time that I didn't mean to do that. I've wanted to do that all day."

"I know. Me too." She was shaking all over, one part of her wanting to rush back into his arms, the other part wanting to run.

"I knew I wanted to kiss you," he said. "And I

knew I shouldn't. But I walked you home—and kissed you—anyway."

"I didn't exactly resist." Her resistance to Garth had held about as firm as a puff of dandelion seeds in a strong breeze.

Garth reached out and touched her cheek gently, tracing a tender path along her jaw before dropping his hand. "No, but knowing you feel the same way doesn't make it easier. You have your dreams, and I . . ."

Kelly stared at him. She knew—*she knew*—what he was trying to say. Knew as well as he did that no matter how perfectly she fit into his arms, she didn't fit into his life. What he needed and what she wanted were poles apart.

"Maybe it's just chemistry," he continued. "Maybe it's something more. Either way, it doesn't matter, does it?"

"No, it doesn't matter," she made herself say. But she knew it wasn't just chemistry.

"We should stay away from each other for a while. Because if we don't . . ."

He didn't have to finish the sentence. She knew what he was saying. He couldn't resist her any more than she could resist him. They'd almost kissed each other in the middle of the park today, in front of half the town. That was what happened when they were together.

She took a deep breath and nodded. "That's probably a good idea." She put her key in the lock with trembling fingers. After pushing open the door, she flicked on the light switch, then stood there, resting her hand on the doorknob, wanting him to go and not wanting him to go. "You'd better go," she managed.

And so he did.

# NINE

For the next few days Kelly immersed herself in work, taking on extra hours, and made arrangements with friends to go to the movies or shopping after work. She decided to fly to St. Kitts the next weekend when a special deal for travel agents came up. Distraction was what she needed, and lots of it. Somehow, some way, she had let Garth and his girls get under her skin.

And somehow, some way, she was going to get him back *out* from under her skin.

She wouldn't be sidetracked from her plans. When Brian and Beth had needed her, she hadn't had a choice. But she had a choice now. She wasn't going to get involved with Garth and his family. A little neighborly concern was one thing. But nothing else was allowed.

Of course, concern didn't explain those kisses. But that was where hormones played their part, and she was mature enough to accept that and move on. Clearly, Garth understood that their kisses were mistakes. He had been the one to say they should keep their distance for a while.

*Why hadn't she been the one to say that?* Embarrassment flooded her every time she thought about her own weakness.

Thanksgiving was coming up soon, and it was a welcome diversion. The twins would be coming home for the long holiday weekend. And in just another month she had her big Christmas trip to the Caribbean.

She met her friends for lunch the Thursday before Thanksgiving to go over plans for the cruise.

"I am absolutely curling up with envy." Stephanie Kelman sighed as she gazed at the cruise brochures spilled across the restaurant table. Stephanie had originally planned to go on the cruise, but after a whirlwind courtship a few months before, she'd gotten married and was already expecting a child. She was small-boned and slender, and was so excited about being pregnant that she was already wearing maternity clothes.

"Oh, sure. You're gloriously happy with Mr. Right and you know it." Jenna Halston's auburn bob swished about her cheeks as she shook her head. "I'd trade places with you in a second."

"Maybe you'll meet someone on the cruise," Diane Jarvis put in, her light eyes sympathetic. Her longish face was framed by straight blond hair.

"Easy for you to say," Jenna pointed out. "You've been dating Jeff for almost a year."

"Kelly's the one we really have to worry about," Stephanie said. "When's the last time you had a date?"

Kelly shrugged. "I don't know," she answered honestly, not liking where the topic of conversation was heading.

The waitress arrived just in time to rescue her from followup commentary from her friends, and they placed their orders. Then the waitress left, and Kelly was relieved when Stephanie passed around an ultrasound picture of her baby, diverting the conversation.

"It looks like a kidney bean," Diane joked, and handed the picture to Kelly.

She stared at the fuzzy black-and-white picture. She felt a yearning in her heart.

She'd never experienced maternal urges before. She'd sort of assumed she wasn't going to have them, that raising her brother and sister had filled that space inside her.

So why did she suddenly feel this longing?

She passed the picture to Jenna and shook off the strange sensation.

"Speaking of men—and aren't I always?—I heard that cute new vet moved into your neighborhood," Jenna said, her gaze flicking from the picture to Kelly. "I took my dog in for shots last week. Talk about handsome." She passed it back to Stephanie.

"Actually, he lives next door." Kelly regretted her admission right away when her friends' expressions turned speculative.

"Lucky you," Jenna said. "An eligible hunk right next door. How convenient."

"He has four kids," Kelly pointed out.

"Hmm." Jenna didn't look convinced that this was a problem. "So, here's what we know about him so far. He's a hunk. He has a great job. He loves children and animals. Yes, I see the problem." Her voice dripped sarcasm.

"Oh, I know who you're talking about!" Stephanie said suddenly. "I've seen him. He's drop-dead gorgeous."

Kelly didn't need to think about Garth's drop-dead-gorgeous good looks. It only made her think of his sad gentleness. His gruff sensitivity. And, most of all, his hot, sweetly devouring mouth.

"You better not let Tom hear you talking like that," Kelly said, feigning shock and trying her best to get off the subject of Garth.

Stephanie laughed. "You know I adore Tom. But I'm not blind. And last time I checked, neither were you."

"I heard he's really nice," Diane said. "My neighbor took her puppy in to see him."

"Fine." Kelly rolled her eyes. "He's cute. He loves animals and children. He's perfect. He's just not for me—I'm not looking for a heavy relationship, remember?"

"Who said anything about a *heavy* relationship?" Stephanie inquired.

An abrupt silence fell over the table. The clink of silverware and the chatter of the surrounding diners filled the air. The three women stared at Kelly speculatively.

"Absolutely nobody!" Kelly declared firmly. She battled back the urge to tell her friends the truth about her mixed-up feelings for Garth. To confide that she'd kissed him. But they would make too much of it, would dig too deep. Deeper than she was ready to dig. "I didn't mean anything by that. Now, can we talk about something else—like the trip? I want to make reservations for the island excursions in advance. Which ones do you guys want to do?"

She determinedly pointed to the brochures on the table.

"Speed is everything in medicating a cat," Garth explained patiently late Thursday afternoon to the thirtysomething pet owner standing by the table in his examining room. She was attractive, with lustrous nut-brown hair and pretty green eyes.

She taught first grade and she'd made a not-too-subtle point of letting him know she was single. He'd treated the cat on Monday, and she'd been in every day since, claiming she couldn't administer the prescribed pills.

The receptionist had reported to Garth that

she'd inquired into his marital status, and he had a hunch there might be more behind her daily appearances in his examining room than timidity over medicating her pet.

There was no reason he shouldn't ask her out. He was thinking about dating, after all. He didn't think Rebecca Whitney would turn him down. The receptionist had even told her about his four children and the news apparently had not turned her off.

"I'll go over the pilling procedure again," he said to her. She moved closer, brushing against him, her delicate flowery scent surrounding his senses.

He felt nothing. No awareness. No out-of-control desire. He didn't want to kiss the living daylights out of her.

*He wanted to kiss the living daylights out of Kelly.*

"Place the cat on a counter or table," he went on, his mind lurching distractedly from the subject at hand to the oddness of his nonreaction to Rebecca Whitney. "Face him in the same direction as you are and get up behind him."

*If his hunger for Kelly was only the symptom of repressed physical need, why didn't he hunger for Rebecca Whitney? She was beautiful and available . . . and far more appropriate.*

He pulled Rebecca's cat, Mugs, against him. "Hug him to you with one arm and with the other hand press his mouth open." He demonstrated the technique. "Quickly put the pill in the middle of his tongue and close his mouth. That's all there is to it." He stroked the cat's throat until Mugs swallowed the medication.

"Oh, Dr. Holloway, you are so good at that." Rebecca smiled at him, displaying a set of glorious white teeth. "I don't know why I can't do it. Mugs just responds so well to you. You must have the magic touch." She smiled some more. "Thank you so much."

Garth handed the wriggling cat to his owner and backed around the examining table. "You have one more day of medication," he said.

"I'll try to do it myself, but I hope you won't mind if I have to come in again."

"That's fine."

Rebecca smiled yet again, then slipped Mugs into a blue plastic pet carrier. The feline instantly set up a mewling protest.

"Let me get that for you," Garth offered, and picked up the carrier. He led the way out of the examining room to the waiting area.

"Thank you," Rebecca said when he carried the pet outside to the parking lot. She showed him to a red compact. "You're Carrie's dad, aren't you?" she asked, unlocking her car. She opened the rear driver's-side door and he set the carrier on the seat.

"That's right." He shut the door.

"She's in the class across the hall from me— Mrs. Guthrie's second-grade class. She's a sweet girl. You have four, don't you?"

"That's right."

"I love kids." She gazed at him hopefully.

Ask her out, you idiot, he railed to himself. But he couldn't do it. No matter how gorgeous Rebecca Whitney was, he didn't feel anything when she smiled at him.

"Good luck with Mugs," he said.

Rebecca looked slightly disappointed as she got into her car. Garth walked back inside the clinic, depressed suddenly. It was time to pick up Toby, then the rest of the girls, and head for the grocery store.

He knew he wouldn't spend a second of the evening alone, yet he felt lonely already.

"Cleanup on aisle twelve," blared a voice over the loudspeaker at the supermarket. Kelly pushed her cart around the corner of aisle eleven and into aisle twelve and nearly crashed into another cart.

"Garth." She blinked, frozen for a second.

He looked just as drop-dead gorgeous as Stephanie had described him. He was the epitome of tall, dark, and handsome. Why did he have to go around looking so good all the time?

She tried really hard to be irritated with him for that, but when she spoke, her voice came out sounding breathless. "What are you doing here?"

Instantly, she felt idiotic. Duh! He was in a grocery store.

He stared at her. "Grocery shopping."

She blushed to the roots of her hair. She tried

to focus on the tableau around him, battling to rein in the giddy awareness that was making mincemeat of her brain. Toby was hanging off one side of the cart while Carrie hung off the other. Michelle and Liza were arguing over control of the cart's handle. Garth had a list in his hand and a harried look on his face. Broken glass and juice puddled the floor in the middle of aisle twelve.

Carrie hopped off the cart and ran to wrap her arms around Kelly's waist. "Toby broke two jars of juice," she announced, gazing up at Kelly with her shining dark eyes.

"I see that," Kelly murmured.

An employee with a mop appeared and began cleaning up the mess. Garth looked embarrassed.

"I think we've made our presence known," he said dryly. "Michelle crashed the cart into a display of cans at the front of the store when we first arrived too. I'm hoping we can make it out of here without blowing up the building."

"Oh." Kelly suppressed a grin. "Well, there's something about grocery stores and kids, you know. It's like entering the Twilight Zone. Normally well-behaved children turn into monsters from the deep when you're in a supermarket."

"Yeah, but I'm always hoping for a miracle," he said.

He smiled, and her heart gave a lurch. She had time to gather her wits again while he apologized to the supermarket employee.

The employee left, and Garth turned back to her.

"We're laying in supplies for this weekend," Garth said. "We're going camping. I want to take advantage of this warm weather while it lasts."

"Great. I hope you have a wonderful time." She was ridiculously pleased that he'd followed up on her suggestion.

She noticed that Liza didn't look particularly thrilled, but the other girls were clearly excited, and she hoped for Garth's sake that the trip would turn out well.

An older woman tried to enter the aisle, and Kelly moved her cart to the side. Liza moved their cart. Carrie let go of Kelly's waist and climbed onto the side of their cart again.

"Can Kelly go camping with us?" Michelle asked.

Kelly's gaze flashed to Garth. His eyes shone with something unfathomable. *Regret?*

"No," he said in a firm voice. "She can't."

The memory of the night of the festival stretched almost tangibly between them and the decision they had made to keep their distance. A flash of regret stabbed at her.

"Why can't Kelly come with us?" Carrie pressed.

"You need family time, just you and your dad," Kelly explained. Suddenly she felt as if she was an outsider, and it was painful and confusing. "And I'm going to be in St. Kitts this weekend, anyway."

"What's St. Kitts?" Toby asked.

"It's an island, sweetie. In the Caribbean Sea." Kelly forced a breezy smile. "I'd better get going now. We're causing a traffic jam." She gave the girls a wave and nodded to Garth.

*Distance. Distance.* She needed to keep her distance from this man.

She pushed her cart blindly down the aisle. She was finally free. A man with Garth's responsibilities should give her the willies—big time.

What was wrong with her?


"There's smoke coming out of the house next door!" Beth exclaimed.

Kelly rushed to the window. It was Thanksgiving afternoon. The turkey was in the oven. Football was on TV. The twins were home.

And there was smoke coming out of Garth's house.

"Oh, no." She ran outside in nothing but her stockinged feet, jeans, and a blouse, heedless of the frosty weather.

She dashed across the yard, noting the smoke was coming from Garth's kitchen window. Then the front door of the house opened and Garth burst outside, more smoke billowing from a pan in his oven-mitted hands.

He bolted down the steps and, with one strong heave, tossed out the contents of the pan. Something large and blackened rolled over the grass and came to a stop at the foot of a large pecan tree.

Kelly blinked, her gaze swerving to Garth. His children rushed out onto the porch. Brian and Bethany arrived on the scene shortly afterward.

"What happened?" Kelly gasped.

A look of shock came over his face and she realized that he hadn't even noticed her until she spoke.

"Daddy burned the turkey!" Michelle cried.

The girls walked over to their father.

"I told him he couldn't broil it, but he wouldn't listen to me," Liza told Kelly. "He won't let me cook because he thinks I'll set the house on fire. Ha! He's the one that started a fire!"

"Should I call the fire department?" Kelly asked.

"No! No one needs to call the fire department," Garth said, his mouth set with annoyance. He was still holding the pan, his hands protected by thick oven mitts. "The house isn't on fire. Everything is fine. Perfectly fine."

"I can see that." Kelly lifted her brows in disbelief. Crossing her arms, she absently rubbed her hands up and down her upper arms to fight the chilly air. "So everything is fine and you always wanted a turkey decorating your lawn, is that it?"

"Well, the turkey was on fire," Garth clarified tersely. "But only briefly."

"How did it happen?" Kelly waited for his answer. Brian and Bethany watched with interest while the girls stared at the charred turkey, their faces glum.

Garth sighed. "I forgot to take it out of the freezer until this morning."

"Ah. It takes days for a turkey to defrost, which should be done in the refrigerator, by the way," Kelly told him.

"I cooked it for a few hours," Garth went on, "but we were getting hungry and it still seemed frozen, so I thought if I broiled it for a little while . . ."

Kelly bit the inside of her cheek to stifle the laughter that was struggling to burst free. "That's not a good idea."

"Oh, thanks for that news flash!" Garth said dryly. "Anyway, somehow the juices caught on fire under the broiler."

"There were big flames!" Carrie said, her eyes round.

"Thank goodness no one was hurt," Kelly said.

"I threw a bowl of water on it, then it smoked like crazy." His features tightened another fraction. "I opened the window, but the house was filling up with smoke, so I threw the stupid thing out here. I probably shouldn't have done that—maybe I could have saved it." He frowned at the doubtful looks cast his way by his kids. "I was a little frustrated, you might say. End of story. This is embarrassing. I'm sure you have your own holiday to get back to, and we'll get back to ours. It's cold out here."

"But what will you do for a turkey?" Beth asked.

The girls turned four pairs of forlorn brown eyes on their father.

"We won't have a turkey now," Michelle said, tears pooling in her eyes.

Carrie suddenly burst into tears. "We can't have Thanksgiving!"

Toby started crying too. "I want a drumstick!" she wailed.

Even Liza's eyes looked red and shiny.

"Thanksgiving isn't about turkeys," Garth said, his voice tinged with exasperation. "It's about being thankful. We can be plenty thankful without a turkey. Or we can go out to a restaurant."

"Oh, no," Beth protested. "Come eat with us. We have a huge turkey. We have loads of food."

Kelly's gaze darted to Garth, then to Beth. Her little sister stared back at her with a satisfied smirk.

Toby ran and clamped her arms around Kelly's legs.

"Oh, please, Daddy, can we?" Carrie begged tearfully.

Garth looked uneasy. "Girls—"

"We would be happy to have you join us," Kelly said. She felt uneasy, too, and trapped. Since Beth had already spoken, she could do nothing but second the invitation.

"We can't possibly intrude on your holiday," Garth argued.

"Thanksgiving is about family and friends. It's

no intrusion at all," Kelly said. "You're our neighbors. Our *friends.*" She emphasized the word *friends* carefully. Garth's gaze met hers squarely, the same incredible energy crackling between them, putting the lie to her words. Her heartbeat quickened; her mouth dried. She felt so very vulnerable.

Could she really be friends with a man who looked at her like *this*, made her feel like *that?*

"All right," Garth said. He stared at her for another long moment. "Thank you." He shifted his attention to the girls. "We'll pack up the rest of the food—the corn, the green beans, and the ice cream—and go over to Kelly's."

"Yay!" The girls dashed into the house, Garth following behind them.

Kelly headed back home with Brian and Beth. At the most, she had five minutes before the Holloways descended.

Five minutes to set five more places at the table, berate Beth for her matchmaking, and remind her foolish heart that Garth could never be more than a friend.

# TEN

Entering Kelly's house was like being enveloped in a warm embrace. The instant Garth stepped inside, the sounds and smells reached out, grabbed him, drew him in. There was no resisting it.

Even if he wanted to. Which he didn't.

He'd tried, for a solid second or two, to tell himself that he'd agreed to Thanksgiving at Kelly's for the kids' sake. But the lie was too huge.

He wanted to be there, to be with Kelly. He was tired of pretending that he didn't. Kelly was a fierce, hot ache inside him that wouldn't go away, no matter how hard he tried to avoid seeing her or thinking about her.

The only question now was—what next?

He didn't have an answer.

The girls flocked ahead of him into the house, Beth holding the door wide as she welcomed them in. The cheerful beat of Christmas music from the stereo competed with the dull roar of a televised football game. Along with the noise came layer after layer of aromas—pumpkin pie, baked apples, turkey, fresh bread.

And then there was the laughter, the chatter, the sheer energy of his children as they swarmed inside.

"We've got books and puzzles and games," Beth said as she directed the girls to a built-in cabinet behind the sofa in the den. The kids followed her.

Brian was stretched out on a recliner in front of the TV. "Need some help with that?" He got up and nodded at the wrapped food Garth was carrying.

"Thanks. I'm all right. I know where the kitchen is," Garth told him. He headed that way and found Kelly at the sink, peeling potatoes. Her honey hair swept around her shoulders, glimmering in the overhead fluorescent light.

She turned, smiled shyly. Garth felt an answering pull in his gut.

"Hi. Um, just put that stuff on the counter, thanks." She shifted her attention to the food in his arms, then pushed a wayward strand of hair back off her cheek. "Go ahead and watch the game, enjoy yourself. I've got everything under control here." She waved him off.

"I'd rather help," Garth said, setting the food down. "Unless you don't want me to." He studied her. "Is it going to make you uncomfortable if I stay in here and help you?" he asked directly. He knew being in the same room with her made *him* uncomfortable. It was a tantalizing, *terrifying* kind of uncomfortable that he couldn't walk away from.

He'd already tried walking away from it. That hadn't worked. Maybe it was time to try a new tack, time to deal with this attraction head-on.

Kelly was staring at him, looking startled by his question. "Of course I'm not uncomfortable. I was just thinking I would have to put the fire department on standby now."

"Beautiful *and* funny," he said dryly.

Something flickered far back in her eyes, but before he could identify it, it was gone.

"I guess you could do the potatoes," she said briskly, all business. "That would help."

He moved to the sink, his fingers closing over hers as he slipped the potato peeler from her hand to his. The exchange of electricity was so strong, it shuddered through his entire body.

She had to have felt it too.

The peeler clattered into the sink, neither of them managing to hold on to it.

"Sorry." She backed up, retreating from the contact.

"How was St. Kitts?" he asked, giving them both breathing space by changing the subject.

"Fine. I love the beach." She moved to inspect the food he'd brought. "So how was camping?" She began unpacking the vegetables and fruit as he picked up the peeler and set to work peeling potatoes. The *flick-flick* of skin flying off the potato into the sink filled the air.

"It went great." He described his weekend at the state park with the kids. "I'm not sure anything really changed because we went on the trip, but I don't think we've felt like a family unit like that in a long time. No TV, no radio, no big house for everyone to separate into different rooms. We spent the whole weekend together—doing everything from putting up the tent to hiking. Liza was the least thrilled to be there, of course, but I think she came around by the end of the weekend. She actually asked when we could go again. She probably wouldn't admit it, but I think she had fun. I know I did."

Kelly tucked the ice cream he'd brought over into her freezer and pushed the door shut. "Then maybe something *did* change," she said softly.

"Maybe." He could only pray that his relationship with his prickly daughter was on the upswing. "I made an appointment with a family counselor here," he told her. "I know Liza still has a lot of feelings inside that she's having trouble dealing with. They all do." He looked at her. "I was looking forward to Thanksgiving. I really wanted to make this a memorable one."

Her mouth quirked as she set about checking various items simmering on the stovetop. "Oh, I don't think the flaming turkey will be forgotten anytime soon." Her expression sobered. "After my parents died, I always made a really big deal out of holidays. Still do, really. I guess I'm still trying to make up for my parents not being here. But, you know, I can't ever completely make up for what we're missing. My parents weren't here, aren't here, and all the pies and cookies and casseroles in the world aren't going to change that. Same for your girls. What matters is the love you show them, the time you spend with them."

Garth nodded. "You're right. I know that. It's hard not to overcompensate, though."

She crossed the kitchen and pulled a serving bowl out of a cabinet by the sink. "You don't need to overcompensate. You're a good father."

"Thank you," he said, feeling she'd paid him a great compliment but knowing at the same time that it wasn't enough, that it wasn't what he wanted from her. That he couldn't keep standing there, not two feet from her, having this nice little conversation that was hardly more than what he could have with his receptionist at the clinic.

"Is that . . ." He had to ask. He had to *know*. There was suddenly nothing more important in the entire universe than the question of whether or not Kelly wanted him the way he wanted her. What he was going to do with the information, he hadn't the slightest idea. He only knew he had to have it, had to know if she had been as unsuccessful in putting him out of her mind as he had been in putting her out of his. "Is that the only way you see me, the only way you think of me?"

"I don't know what you're asking." Was that

really her voice sounding so shaky, so whispery? She'd been trying very hard to act cool, to act as though having Garth and his kids over for Thanksgiving was no big deal.

Only it *was* a big deal. He'd blown her composure to bits the second he'd walked into the kitchen.

She'd lied when she'd told him that having him stay and help her wouldn't make her uncomfortable. Everything about Garth made her uncomfortable. Dizzy. Aware.

*Hot.*

"Am I just the guy next door, a good father, a neighbor, a friend?"

"You're all those things," she said, trying her best to sound rational and collected, to sound like everything that she wasn't.

"I'm also a man."

Kelly's knees trembled. "I had noticed that." Had she ever noticed *that*!

Garth put the peeler on the counter, picked up a dishtowel, and wiped his hands. He turned and leaned against the counter. His gaze drank her in, wouldn't let her move away.

"I've been thinking about dating again."

"Oh."

Why was he having this conversation with her? It had been his idea to put some distance between them. Then it hit her. Maybe he wanted her to help him out, set him up on a date. She was so wrapped up in her own little world, where his very nearness sent her into a tailspin, that she was forgetting he didn't necessarily feel the same way.

Sure, he'd been attracted to her for a minute or so. Long enough for one or two kisses. But he'd gotten over it.

Jenna. Her friend's name slipped neatly into her mind. She could set him up with Jenna.

She tried hard to open her mouth and make the suggestion, but she couldn't. A sharp pain in the region of her heart prevented her.

Jealousy, she realized abruptly. When she thought of Jenna with Garth, she was consumed by the green monster.

"Good for you," she said firmly, pushing down her contrary emotions. "Sounds like a great idea." Deciding she'd had enough of this confusing conversation, she stepped away from him, setting the serving bowl down on the counter. She took a can of cranberry sauce out of the pantry and opened it, then spooned it into the dish.

Garth went back to the potatoes. "I'm glad you like the idea," he said after several minutes, his gaze remaining fixed on his task. He finished, and after filling up a pot with water and the potatoes, he carried it over to the stove.

Kelly switched on the burner as he set the pot down.

"So where do you want to go?" he asked.

"What are you talking about?" He'd thrown her for a loop.

"On our date. Where do you want to go?"

"Me?" She heard herself squeak and struggled to control her voice, shock and excitement washing over her. "You can't ask me for a date." It wasn't sensible. It wasn't careful. It wasn't in her plans. She worked to recall the reason why she couldn't go on a date with him. Her mind was traitorously fuzzy on that point all of a sudden. Instead, the message "He wants *me*" kept blinking in her consciousness, overriding everything else. "We decided—"

"Maybe we were wrong." Garth knew what she was going to say. They'd decided the night of the festival to keep their distance from each other.

He knew he'd shocked her. He'd shocked himself. He couldn't believe he was asking her out on a date. It was crazy, dangerous. And he was doing it anyway.

"Garth—"

Carrie chose that moment to skip into the kitchen, singing a silly Thanksgiving song. She giggled as she finished the song and plopped into a seat at the table.

Toby followed her. She had a worn doll in her arms. Garth supposed it must be one of Kelly's or Beth's old toys. She climbed into a seat by her sister.

"When will dinner be ready?" Carrie asked. "I'm hungry."

"Soon," Kelly said, obviously distracted as she moved to set the cranberry sauce in the microwave.

Garth watched her curiously. She stood there

for several seconds, staring at the microwave before opening it and retrieving the cranberry sauce. Then she went to the refrigerator and put the dish inside.

Garth didn't remark on her strange behavior. He was feeling pretty off-balance himself.

He decided to give them both a little time to recoup. It wouldn't be wise for either of them to rush into anything.

Not that he planned to wait very long. But he could at least wait until after dinner. After all, he didn't want her so distracted that she set her turkey on fire too.

"I'm going to catch some of the game," he said. "We'll talk later."

She bit her lip and stared at him. He wanted to kiss her, and he wondered if she could possibly know how hard it was for him to walk away without taking her sweet face into his hands and doing just that. But he'd promised himself not to rush.

He wasn't sure how long he could keep that promise.

"Thank you, God, for the food you set in the forest. Amen." Toby unfolded her hands and grabbed the drumstick on her plate, her big eyes alight with anticipation as she sank her teeth into the turkey leg.

Kelly stared at her curiously, still trying to figure out the little girl's prayer.

"That's 'the food you set before us' in Toby language," Liza whispered to Kelly.

"Oh." Kelly smiled as she surveyed the family scene before her—the chaos of a dining room full of hungry kids reaching for this, passing that, laughing and chattering, warmed her. She realized how good it was to have the room so full and how easily Garth's family blended with hers.

For the holiday she'd brought out the best of everything—her parents' silver, china, and crystal. An heirloom white lace cloth covered the table and tall tapers burned in the brass candlesticks. Strains of "Rudolph the Red-Nosed Reindeer" drifted in from the stereo in the den.

Across the table, Garth's eyes met hers. Their kitchen conversation hovered in the air between them. *Maybe we were wrong.* He watched her, his dark eyes serious, intense. *We'll talk later.* Her heart fluttered madly.

Garth still wanted her. He hadn't effortlessly pushed her out of his mind. He was having second thoughts about their decision to stay away from each other. He didn't want her to set him up with one of her friends.

He wanted *her*.

The knowledge was seductive, intoxicating. Frightening and thrilling.

What was going to happen now?

She had a feeling that they were headed toward the edge of a cliff. Was she going to run for safety or jump off? She wasn't sure, and as long as they were surrounded by her brother and sister plus his four kids, there wasn't going to be much opportunity to finish the conversation, anyway.

But knowing there was no obvious chance to take up the discussion again didn't help her to get it out of her mind—not with Garth sitting right across the table from her. Not that she thought space would help. She'd gone all the way to St. Kitts the weekend before and hadn't been able to get him out of her mind. No way was she going to get him out of her mind when he was in the same house with her.

Luckily, everyone was so busy eating and talking that no one noticed that she barely ate or spoke during the meal. When it was over, everyone pitched in to carry the dishes back to the kitchen. Brian and Garth insisted on washing up while Kelly put her feet up in the den.

*As if she could relax.*

Her whole body hummed with nervous anticipation. She hadn't forgotten the determined glint in Garth's eyes when he'd said they'd talk later. If an opportunity didn't present itself, she had the feeling that Garth would make one.

It turned out that he didn't have to. By the time the guys finished the dishes and came back to the den, it was growing dark outside. The kids were sprawled on the floor watching TV. Garth sat down on the couch next to Kelly. It was a huge couch and there was plenty of room, but he sat right beside her so that his leg brushed hers.

He leaned back casually, sliding his arm along the back of the couch behind her. She looked at him—huge mistake. His gaze burned into her, liquefying her from the inside out.

And suddenly she wondered if she was kidding herself to think that there was some decision to be discussed, some decision that hadn't already been made. What was happening between her and Garth felt as unstoppable as the rotation of the planet.

"The new Disney movie's playing at the Royal Theater," Beth commented. "How about Brian and I take the kids to go see it? Would that be okay with you, Garth? That would give you and Kelly a chance to unwind."

Kelly stared at Beth. Wisely, Beth didn't meet her sister's eyes.

The three younger girls couldn't wait to go and even Liza seemed interested in going. Kelly had noticed the teenager's admiration of Beth, and if it weren't that the idea of being left alone with Garth had her nervous as all get out, she would be pleased to see them spend more time together. Since Beth was close to Liza's age, she had a feeling her sister could be a positive influence on Garth's eldest daughter.

"I think it's a great idea," Garth said. "Thanks." He removed his arm from the back of the couch and pulled his wallet from his pocket. The four kids gathered around as he started doling out cash.

Words of protest wedged in Kelly's throat. She could insist on going to the movie with them. Or she could stay right where she was—alone, with Garth.

Beth might be doing a little manipulating, but she was in control of her own life, Kelly reminded herself. She didn't have to let herself be alone with Garth.

*But she wanted to be alone with Garth.*

She couldn't remember a time when a man had ever made her feel like Garth made her feel. Like a woman. Like a passionate, desirable woman.

*She wanted to make love to Garth.*

"Have fun, guys," Garth said.

The girls were heading toward the door, Brian and Beth herding them along. Garth was watching her, his knowing eyes dark and devouring. And she was just sitting there, staring back at him. He wanted to make love to her too. She knew it.

All this tension between them—this awful, glorious *hungering*—had been bound to come to a crisis at some point. Maybe it was time to let it happen. She could spend a few hours alone with him. . . .

She could make love to him. . . .

And she could discover that he was just a man. A mere mortal. Her hunger would be sated. She could get on with her life.

*Yeah, right.*

"We'll stop for ice cream afterward," Brian said

from the door. "So don't expect us back for several hours."

Then the door shut and the sounds of the children clattering down the sidewalk faded into silence. They were alone.

Kelly stood up. It was all happening too fast. She had to think. All Garth had really done was ask her for a date. She wasn't even sure going on a date with him was wise, and here she was thinking about having sex with him. And she thought she was in *control*?

"I put some leftovers together for you to take home," she said. "I'll get them for you." She escaped to the kitchen.

Garth flicked off the TV and followed her. She was hauling wrapped leftovers out of the refrigerator and loading them onto the counter. Then she took out a couple of grocery sacks and started packing up the food. Her movements were quick, jerky.

"I can't believe how much we all ate," she said breezily.

Her gaze flashed up to meet his and the apprehensive shimmer in her eyes belied her light tone. He understood. He felt it too—the fight-or-flight adrenaline that signaled something big was at stake.

"No one ever accused my girls of being small eaters," he said lightly, carefully matching his tone to hers. "I'm just glad none of your china or crystal was broken. It was brave of you to leave it out when you found out we were coming over."

"My mom always believed in using the good stuff," Kelly explained. "Things got broken, but that was okay with her. She never got mad. She said it gave a dish character to have a chip or a fracture line after being repaired. So it never occurred to me to put anything away when I found out you would be joining us."

"Thanks for letting us crash dinner."

She shrugged. "You're welcome. I, uh, I'll help you carry this stuff home." She grabbed a bag and headed for the door.

They were quiet as they crossed the yard, spurred on by the chilly evening air. Once inside his house, they set the sacks down on the table in the kitchen.

"Wait," Garth said when Kelly turned as if she was going to leave.

He couldn't let her go. Later was *now*, and what they had to talk about couldn't wait.

"Don't go yet," he said quietly. "We haven't finished our conversation."

# ELEVEN

"Maybe that's best," Kelly said. "Maybe this is one conversation that shouldn't be finished." She wanted—and didn't want—to have this conversation with Garth.

He stood there, under the blaze of fluorescent light, his dark eyes burning into her, making her feel naked, as if he knew all her secret thoughts. As if he understood them even better than she did.

"I think this is one conversation that we *have* to finish," he said.

"Why?"

"Because I can't get you out of my mind. I tried. I really tried. But I can't do it."

She couldn't bear his scrutiny another second. She spun around, desperate, panicking. But she couldn't convince her traitorous legs to take her out of his house and away from him.

"I see you, feel you, taste you in my dreams"

came his soft, husky voice, dangerously close to her ear. Then his fingers touched her neck, pushing back her hair and brushing fire across her skin.

"Oh, Garth . . ." she whispered.

"I know you're scared." He trailed his hand down along her shoulder, prodding her to face him. "I'm scared too." She turned and he touched her cheek with a tender stroke before dropping his hand to his side.

"You are?" She stared up at him.

"Scared to death," he admitted. "I don't know what I'm feeling right now, I just know that it's so powerful that I can't eat or sleep or breathe without thinking about you. I know we said we should keep our distance, but I can't."

Kelly's heart leaped. She felt a hot rush of emotion inside. Words failed her.

"What I have to know is if you feel the same way," he continued quietly.

"Yes," she said, because she couldn't lie to him, not when he looked at her with such naked longing in his eyes. She ached for him, whether or not it was wise or careful or anything else. It was real, and that was all that mattered.

Then he reached for her and with one forward motion, she was there, in his arms. Soft and gentle and sweet, he kissed her. He pulled her closer, deepening the kiss, sweeping away her doubts. In her heart she felt a rightness, and that was enough for now. Her mind didn't have to comprehend it.

Garth had never desired a woman like he desired Kelly. Hungrily, he moved his mouth from hers to spread kisses across her cheeks, her chin, her neck, her earlobes. She moaned deep in her throat as he cupped one of her full breasts in his hand through her blouse. Need, wild and delirious, surged through him.

"I want you, Kelly." He was stating the obvious. He knew his hardened body, pressed against hers, proclaimed his arousal. Still, he had to give her the chance to slow things down if that was what she wanted.

Her lashes fluttered up as she met his gaze. Passion shone and swirled in her eyes. "I want you too." Her voice was tremulous yet certain at the same time.

They came together again, this time for a fierce, blazing kiss, a kiss that wasn't careful or controlled. It was euphoric. His tongue plundered her mouth, and she answered him just as frantically. He nearly lifted her off the ground, crushing her to his chest, and still she wasn't close enough.

He swept her up into his arms. She buried her face against his shoulder, clinging to him, as he carried her up the stairs to his room. Once inside, he turned the lock in the door, just to be on the safe side, and carried her to the bed. Then he lowered her onto it with utter care and, perching beside her, leaned over her.

Fingers shaking, he unbuttoned her blouse and revealed her lace-covered breasts. He could barely breathe. In the dim room, illuminated only by the muted streetlight cutting between the trees and through the upper-story window, he stared at the perfection of Kelly's rounded breasts. He reached for her, held paradise in one hand. She sighed as he slid his fingers inside the thin material of her bra to tease the hard bud of her nipple. Then she was touching him, fumbling with his pants, tugging at his zipper.

Anticipation thrilled through his bloodstream as she succeeded in opening his pants. She reached for him, grasped him through the thin barrier of his briefs. He groaned in pleasure, and she laughed as she pulled him all the way down beside her. Eagerly, she pushed at his clothes, stroking him, driving him insane.

"Take them off," she ordered, her voice seductive and low.

"Bossy," he teased, nearly delirious by her eager assault. He was giddy with longing. His heart raced; his muscles shivered. Obediently, he peeled his jeans and briefs down his legs and tossed them on the floor, then quickly added his shoes, socks, and shirt to the pile.

His attention returned to Kelly. Not waiting for him, she twisted the front clasp of her bra and her breasts sprang free, pale and perfect. Instinct and need took over. Garth buried his face in the soft mounds. She wrapped her arms around his head, gripping her fingers in his short hair, moaning as he teased and taunted her nipples. He suckled and pulled until she arched intimately against him, writhing. He moved to claim her mouth, his senses spinning.

She was still fully clothed and he couldn't stand it any longer. It was all he could do not to rip her blouse and jeans off. Abruptly he pulled away. Her eyes, filled with fevered heat and hunger, followed him as he swept her bra and blouse back. With a firm hand behind her back, he helped her to raise up just enough to pull the clothing from beneath her and off. She slipped off her shoes and socks as he unfastened her jeans, pushed them down, and whisked off her panties. And then they were both naked. She closed her hand over his rock-hard arousal. He gasped, then groaned.

"Kelly, I want this to last all night, but I don't think it's going to last two seconds if you keep doing that."

A laugh bubbled up out of Kelly's throat, and Garth planted a deep, soul-wrenching kiss on her mouth. His fingers slipped inside her tight heat and he played with her, feathering tiny touches in her, gently forcing his way in. At the same time he was sliding his tongue down her chin, her neck, her chest. He drew a nipple into his mouth again as he continued his exquisite torment below. She wriggled with quivery delight, releasing his hardness to wrap her arms around his back, clutching him.

She let out a cry as he rocked her, cradling her body to him. His ministrations were both powerful and tender, sending shock waves of hazy arousal through her body. There was suddenly nothing but Garth, his lips on her breasts, his fingers inside her.

Then he left her abruptly. She felt so cold, so bereft, she could have cried. He scrounged in the darkness in the bedstand drawer.

He returned, and she realized in a foggy flash of gratitude what he'd left her for when he sheathed his arousal in a condom. "Now, back to our regularly scheduled program," he murmured.

Carefully, quickly, he poised himself over her ready warmth and thrust into her. Each delicious jolt brought him closer, and tension mounted inside her to an aching pitch. Her nipples were swollen and tingling, and there was a veritable inferno between her legs. The tremors when they came were nearly blinding. Pulsations of soul-deep ecstasy shuddered through her. Her heart was aching, surging, and somehow through it all she noticed he had stopped moving, was just holding her.

"Don't stop," she breathed, pleading. And he didn't. He drove into her again and again, and as she came down from the first rapturous peak, she felt another one building. This time he joined her, his body shaking, and then he collapsed beside her, breathing roughly, possessively wrapping her tight against him with one arm.

They lay together for a long time, neither of them moving, as if afraid the magic spell would break if they did, both knowing something special had happened. There was no way to deny that truth. Kelly was no virgin, but she had never thought of herself as very sexual either.

Until now.

Until Garth.

She snuggled into his side and he pulled her closer, stroking her hair, whispering to her that she was beautiful and amazing and perfect. She closed her eyes and let herself drift as her body slowly came down from the pounding bliss of their joining.

"Oh, no! What time is it?" Kelly sat straight up in bed. Garth's bed, her startled mind registered, and everything that had happened washed over her in a jumbled, distorted mess of images.

She found the clock by Garth's bed. Nine-thirty. The kids would be home soon!

Garth had fallen asleep too.

"Garth! Garth!"

His eyes flew open.

"The kids will be home any minute. I have to go." She leaped from the bed, from his arms, and grabbed her clothes, running instinctively for the doorway she hoped was a bathroom. It was. She shut the door and flicked on the light.

She was naked. Tousled hair, swollen lips, flushed cheeks met her appraisal. She looked like a wanton.

She remembered everything clearly then. She *was* a wanton. She had cried and screamed and

writhed in an episode of possibly the best sex anyone in the entire Western Hemisphere had ever
known. Quiet, demure, responsible Kelly had been
a wild wanton in the bed of her next-door neighbor.

What was happening to her?

*Garth.*

Garth was happening to her. She'd had incredible sex with him, and now she was naked in his
bathroom. The essentials of his personal grooming
were scattered around the rim of the white pedestal
sink—his deodorant, his toothpaste, his shaving
cream, his razor.

She felt like an intruder on his privacy. His very
male privacy.

Hysterical laughter caught in her throat. After
what they'd just done, she thought seeing his personal grooming products was intimate?

Trembling, she dragged her jeans on, then realized she'd left her panties off. She stripped off the
jeans and this time put her panties on first. Her
fingers were uncoordinated, nearly useless instru-
ments in her effort to button her blouse.

When she opened the door, Garth was standing
by the bed. He snapped his jeans together, leaving
his shirt untucked. The light by the bed was on,
illuminating the rumpled covers where they'd lain
together and—

"I've got to get home," she said, her heart
pounding as she stared at the bed, then at Garth.

She couldn't believe that only a few hours earlier she'd tried to convince herself that making love with Garth would help her get him out of her system. How totally ludicrous! She was standing six feet away from him, yet she still could feel his hands on her body, his breath on her lips, his heat inside her. His scent, his taste, his touch were all embedded in her very soul.

"Kelly." Garth crossed to her, put a firm hand on each of her arms.

She swallowed thickly, stared at him.

"You look upset," he said.

"I—I'm just . . . overwhelmed," she admitted. "I don't know what we're doing, where this is heading—"

"I know how you feel, Kelly. This is overwhelming for me too."

Her lips parted in surprise. She hadn't been thinking about his feelings, hadn't realized he could be as confused, as uncertain as she. In some odd way, it was a relief to find out that he felt the same way.

"I haven't been with a woman since Julia," he confessed.

"Are you . . . are you sorry we did this?" Kelly asked. She waited, her heart in her throat, for his answer.

His eyes held hers. "No, I'm not sorry."

Tears stung at her eyes. She was shocked at how relieved she was to hear that, how much she'd *needed* to hear that—to know he didn't regret what had just happened between them.

No matter how scared she was, she realized she didn't regret it either.

"So . . . what do we do now?" she whispered.

He reached up with one hand and smoothed back the tangled hair that fell forward across her cheek. His knuckles grazed her jawline in a tender caress before he dropped his hand again. "I don't know. We can't pretend this didn't happen, though."

Garth knew there was no backtracking from his perspective. He couldn't erase the last hour. He didn't *want* to erase the last hour. But at the same time he knew they needed to be careful.

There was more at stake than just his and Kelly's happiness.

He had to think of the kids. Kelly had her dream and he had his reality.

Was he kidding himself to think they could make a relationship work? The only thing he knew was he had to find out.

"We'll take things slow," he said. "One day at a time."

"Oh, okay. Slow. Like the way we took things tonight?"

"We'll work on that." He smiled at her, lowered his hands, curling his fingers through hers. "I know this is kind of backwards at this point, but we started out talking about a date. If I can get a babysitter for next weekend, will you go out to dinner with me?"

Kelly stared at him for a few seconds, then laughed.

"Yes," she said. "I'd love to."

# TWELVE

"Does going on a date with Kelly mean you're going to marry her?" Toby asked.

Garth froze, his razor held in midstroke along his jaw.

"No, pumpkin," he said carefully, completing the stroke and dipping the razor in the filled sink. "It doesn't mean that."

Toby, Carrie, and Michelle were all sitting on the edge of the ceramic tub, sucking on lollipops and watching him get ready for his night out with Kelly. Liza was sleeping over at her friend Tammy's house, and the seventeen-year-old daughter of his clinic partner was going to watch the younger girls.

"We're just going to have dinner together," he went on. "That doesn't mean we're going to get married."

"If dating doesn't mean you're going to get married, what does it mean?" Carrie asked.

"It means that we're friends and that we like each other." He reiterated what he'd said when he talked to them about his planned evening with Kelly. The girls had accepted his answer at the time, but apparently questions had been brewing in their minds since then.

"We want to spend some time together, get to know each other better," he said. "Kind of like when you guys meet someone at school that you like and tell me you want to invite her to go skating or to the zoo. Or like Liza going over to Tammy's house tonight. It's a chance to get to know that person better."

He let the water out of the sink, then rinsed and dried his face. He hoped he'd said the right things. It was important that the girls didn't nurture unrealistic expectations about his relationship with Kelly.

"Oh." Toby pulled on her sucker. "Will I get hair on my face when I grow up?" she asked suddenly.

"No, only boys need to shave their faces when they grow up," Garth told her, relieved to see the subject of marriage so easily dismissed.

"Why?" Toby asked.

"Girls shave their legs," Carrie put in.

"Not all girls," Michelle argued. "I saw a lady at the grocery store with hair on her legs."

"Why don't boys shave their legs?" Toby piped up.

The doorbell saved Garth from the conversation. "Becky must be here," he announced. Passing through the bedroom, he picked up his suit jacket and headed downstairs, still grinning at his kids' silliness. The girls pounded down the steps behind him. Becky was a fresh-faced, outgoing girl, and she quickly had the kids rounding up board games. Garth went over some instructions with the babysitter, then whistled as he shut the door and headed for Kelly's.

She was a vision. He'd told her to dress up and she had, in a beautiful berry-colored dress that enhanced her shapely figure. The neckline plunged to an enticing vee, the material curving over her breasts, then hugging her slender waist and the gentle swell of her hips, and stopping just above the knees. She'd put her hair up, fastening it with a silver clip, loose strands softening the style. Kelly literally took his breath away.

"You look stunning." Garth slid his arm around her waist and planted a firm kiss on her lips, pulling her close. "Mmm, you smell good too," he breathed when he released her mouth. The sensation of her body pressed to his was pure heaven. He didn't want to let her go. He'd been waiting ever since Thanksgiving night, being careful not to touch her or kiss her in front of the children.

The children weren't there now.

So he kissed her again, and she looped her arms around his neck, a soft mewling coming from her throat. The sound drove him crazy. He deepened the kiss, sweeping his tongue inside her mouth. Impatient, dizzying need uncoiled from the center of his being.

"We have dinner reservations," he said hoarsely as he wrenched his mouth from hers.

She looked up at him, her eyes wide.

"We'd better go," he said.

"Are you hungry?" she asked.

"Are you?"

"I was just thinking . . ." She chewed on her lip. "I was thinking it was so nice, you know—you have a baby-sitter tonight and it's just us, and restaurants are so full of . . ."

"People?"

"Yeah."

Kelly's cheeks pinkened, her eyes glowed. Garth's heart almost pounded into his throat.

Neither of them moved. They simply stared at each other for several long beats instead. Then he was kissing her again. Somehow, they moved backward, through the entry hall into the den.

"The food isn't that good there, anyway," she whispered breathlessly.

"I never said what restaurant I was taking you to," he pointed out.

"It doesn't matter," she said.

He laughed, then claimed her mouth again. "I

think I remember where the bedroom is," he managed finally between kisses. He slid his arms down her sides, sliding one hand below the hem of her dress and bunching it up to the curve of her bottom. She lifted her leg, curling it around him.

He groaned. "Or maybe we're not going to make it to the bedroom after all."

"I can't wait that long," she said. "I feel like we've been waiting forever as it is." She tore his necktie free from his collar and pulled it off. Reaching for the buttons of his shirt, she unfastened them one after another until she could push the material apart and flatten her hands to his chest. A seductive sigh escaped from her lips as he buried his face in her neck, laving it and nipping at the soft skin with his teeth. Eagerly he shrugged out of his suit jacket and shirt, then went to work on her dress, whisking the zipper down and kissing her shoulder. The garment pooled at her feet, leaving her standing before him in her underclothes.

He twisted open her bra, then knelt to tenderly dispense with her hose and panties, lingering to kiss her thighs, the backs of her knees, her ankles. She shivered beneath his slow, teasing touch until he rose again and just stared at her. She didn't move, let him drink her in. She was so beautiful. He was going to taste her, touch her, drown in her.

"Kelly," he whispered, then whatever he was going to say next was lost as she unbuckled his belt and slipped her hand inside his trousers. He was on fire.

With a careful arm behind her back, balancing her, he nudged her backward onto the couch. She was still fumbling with his pants, unbuttoning them, pushing at them. He helped her get them down, get everything off, including his briefs.

Poised above her, steadying himself with one arm braced against the couch, he leaned in to place his mouth on hers, to savor her sweetness. Gently, she met him with her tongue, outlining his lips with it, boldly but tenderly taking possession of his mouth. He needed more, reaching for the source of her heat, still kissing her. As he found his way between her thighs, she arched upward.

He wrenched his lips from hers. Both of them were breathing raggedly. Her eyes, widened and darkened with unmasked desire, met his. Her honey hair splayed wildly about her.

"I could look at you forever," he said huskily.

"I want you to do more than look," she whispered. Cupping the length of him in her hand, she stroked him, encouraged him.

The sensation of her fingers against him had his heart rate going triple time. He was throbbing, aching, for her. Her legs tightened around his back and she urged him downward. She let go of his erection as his body closed over hers. The hardened tips of her breasts raked his chest. He sank his face into the soft mounds of her chest, sucking and whirling his tongue around each peak. Her hips shifted against him, starting a rhythm, and he just barely remembered in time to grab his pants and find the little foil packet tucked in his billfold.

She watched him, taking in every last detail of his nakedness. When he looked up at her, she smiled, a slow, sure smile. Then, ready, he came back and plunged into her. She cried out, sweetly, needily, and he would have exploded right then if he hadn't held on with exquisite control. Every second inside Kelly was mind-blowing, awesome, incredible.

There was no way sex—sheer, physical sex—could be this good. His heart was involved, no two ways about it.

He moved inside her. She felt slick and hot, lifting her hips to meet him. He wanted the moment to last as long as possible, and with excruciating slowness he slid in and out until she moaned. Unable to stop himself any longer, he picked up the pace. Then she shuddered beneath him and all his fine plans to make their lovemaking last for hours evaporated. He let go, went over the edge of the world with her.

Afterward, carefully, gently, he pulled her over him, taking her weight against him so that he wouldn't crush her on the narrow space of the couch. "I've dreamed of this," he said. "Every night . . ."

"Me too," she whispered against his chest.

They ordered pizza.

When the deliveryman came, Garth put on his pants and shirt, which he left unbuttoned. Kelly slipped on her long terry robe, and they watched a TV movie and ate with great appetite. Afterward, Kelly sat back in a corner of the couch, her feet propped on Garth's lap, watching him. She wasn't paying the slightest bit of attention to the movie. She couldn't have said what the title was.

All she could think about was Garth. She hadn't been with a man in a while, but she wasn't completely inexperienced with relationships. She knew what she was feeling for Garth was different.

She knew that she thought about him all the time, could hardly imagine a day without him anymore. *Was she in love with him?*

She'd never been in love before. Did love explain this delicious *aching* inside her?

"Penny for your thoughts."

She started, then realized he was looking at her. The movie had gone to a commercial. "Uh, I was just thinking about Carrie's costume," she stumbled, making a quick recovery. She'd started working on a princess costume for Carrie. The little girl had a part in her school's holiday play.

"I really appreciate your help with that," Garth said. "I can learn to cook, but I don't think sewing is ever going to be in my bag of tricks. I feel like you're doing a lot more work on your end of our deal than I am, you know."

"Oh, no," Kelly protested. "You've done a lot

for me. You fixed my garbage disposal and put anti-freeze in my car. And just yesterday you cut off that obnoxious branch that kept scratching at my bed-room window, keeping me up nights. Believe me, I don't want to take up tree trimming any more than you want to learn to sew!"

Kelly thought about how easy it was to let Garth slide into her life, take care of her problems. She helped him, too, so she didn't feel dependent. She felt part of a team.

She hadn't gone looking for a relationship, hadn't wanted one. But one had found her anyway.

"How's Santa doing?" She knew Garth had been spending his lunch hours shopping and hid-ing gifts in his attic.

"Almost done," he said. "Of course, they all have to have the hottest toys of the year, so I might have to do a run into the city next week to search out some of the hard-to-find items."

"Where do things stand with the girls' plans for going to see their mom during the holidays?" Garth had told her that Julia had promised to fly the kids out to California.

His mouth tightened. "I haven't heard from Julia again about their travel arrangements, which isn't a good sign. I'm afraid she's going to back out on them."

Kelly's heart ached at the thought of the girls being disappointed that way. "Oh, no." She real-ized in that moment that she wasn't just falling in love with Garth. She was falling in love with Toby, Carrie, Michelle, and Liza too.

She sat up and reached for his hand, wanting to find some way to offer her support.

"It's happened before," he went on. "She makes plans with them, then she backs out. If it were up to me, I wouldn't tell them about the plans till I was sure she was going to follow through, but she calls and tells them she's sending for them, so I don't have any say in it."

The bitter tinge to his voice made Kelly hurt inside. She knew he felt the girls' pain every bit as much as they did.

"I'm so sorry. I hope she ends up coming through. I know how much it would mean to the girls. What are your plans for Christmas if they do go?"

He shrugged. "My parents live in Houston. They're going to my sister's in Florida, and they've invited me to join them. I haven't made any plans, though. I just have a bad feeling because Julia hasn't sent the tickets yet."

"Your girls are so lucky to have you as their dad," Kelly commented softly.

"Thanks."

He squeezed her hand, and Kelly leaned her head against his shoulder. Neither of them said anything for a few minutes. The movie came back on.

"I'm going to admit something," Garth said, and Kelly realized he wasn't paying any more attention to the movie than she was. "I was really nervous about tonight."

Kelly smiled and sat up. She could relate to Garth's comment in a big way. "Really?"

"Yep. *Very* nervous. I haven't been on a date in fifteen years. Not since I was twenty years old!"

Kelly tried to imagine a twenty-year-old Garth. Still gorgeous, but without the hurting eyes. She wished she could have known that Garth. "I bet you were hot stuff," she teased. She folded her knees to her chest and wrapped her arms around her legs. She leaned back against the couch, watching him.

"You'd be wrong," he said. "I was pretty intense about my studies. I didn't really date that much. What about you?"

"Not much to tell. Well, I was the prom queen." At his lifted eyebrows, she added, "Yes, that's my claim to fame, Hope High School prom queen."

"So what happened to the prom king?"

"He runs the feedstore now, the one out on Highway 46. It's a family business. He's married, has two kids."

"How did he let you get away?"

"Oh, Tony and I were just friends," she explained. "I guess I haven't had any relationships in the past that I would really categorize as serious."

She knew for a fact that this was one thing that had changed now. Whatever was happening between her and Garth, it was serious.

"We didn't do a very good job of taking things slow tonight, did we?" she asked suddenly.

Garth didn't know what to say for a minute. He knew she was right. And he knew, too, that if he thought about it very hard, he might have to face all the different ways that their relationship could be hopeless.

And he didn't want it to be hopeless. He wanted to keep trying, keep believing, that they could make it work.

So he said, "We just need more practice," and he turned off the television using the remote control, scooped her up into his arms, carried her upstairs, and showed her how exquisitely slow he could go.

# THIRTEEN

"I've never had so much fun in my whole life," Kelly announced as she walked out of a Dallas comedy club hand in hand with Garth. The neighborhood was filled with bright streetlights and the sounds of conversation and laughter as people milled on the sidewalks. Dallas's West End was alive at night, with a range of theaters, comedy clubs, bars, and tourist shops.

"Never?"

Kelly grinned, a curl of warmth rolling through her. "Okay, scratch that. I've never had more fun *in public* in my whole life. How's that?"

"Better." Garth squeezed her hand.

It had been a week since their last attempt at a real date. This time Garth had insisted they *really* go out. He'd planned a full evening in the city, with dinner reservations followed by the comedy club. Becky was baby-sitting again.

They headed for the car, which was parked a few blocks away. "I wish we didn't have to go back already," Garth said. "But Becky's parents don't like her to be out past midnight."

"It's all right. We have a long drive to Hope, so we'd better get started." She was sorry, though, when they reached the car. She didn't want the evening to end.

"I'm going to miss you next weekend," he said as he nosed the vehicle into traffic, heading out of the busy West End and to the freeway, toward home.

Kelly was going to Playa del Carmen. She'd had the excursion to the Mayan ruins planned for months. Now there was a big part of her that felt oddly reluctant to go.

"I'll miss you too," she said, watching Garth in the darkness of the car. She felt a twinge of regret, thinking of time spent so many miles away from Garth's arms. "But I have to work on my list, you know," she said, half teasingly. "It's hard work, conquering the world."

It occurred to her as she said the words that it *was* hard work. She'd never thought of her dream that way before. Her list of places to go, things to do had always excited her, driven her. She'd started with her parents' list and added to it for years.

The list was awfully long.

"You have your whole life to conquer the world," Garth said quietly. "What's your rush?"

He glanced away from the road for a second and met her eyes.

"I used to think I had lots of time," Kelly replied. "So did my parents, but they didn't. And neither did I. When I was twenty-one, I thought I had all the time in the world to do whatever I wanted. Instead, I ended up at home helping Brian and Beth with their homework, taking them to soccer games and swim meets, and worrying about having enough money to pay for school clothes and groceries. If there's one thing I've learned, it's that you never have as much time as you think you have."

Garth didn't say anything, and they drove in silence for several minutes. The bright lights of the city were behind them. Dark countryside whizzed by.

"I think about my parents a lot," she said softly, staring out into the darkness. "They died, and they never did any of the things they wanted to do. I think that's so sad."

"It's sad if they weren't happy with the way they lived their life during the time they had," Garth pointed out. "Do you think your parents were happy?"

Kelly swung her gaze to his. "I don't know," she said. "I guess so. I just know they missed so much. And I—"

"And you don't want to miss anything."

"Something like that." She was quiet for a minute. "But I don't want to miss *you* either, Garth," she added suddenly. "I feel like I'm being so greedy with you. I don't know if or when I'll ever be ready to settle down. Our lives are going in different directions. Are we crazy?"

"Yes."

His tone was so deadly serious that Kelly felt a little semihysterical bubble of laughter rise up inside. "And you're okay with that?"

"So far," he said. "But what I'm not okay with is you sitting all the way over there." He reached across the vehicle's bench seat, slung his arm around her shoulder, and pulled her toward him. He snuggled her against him, driving with one hand. "I don't care how many places you have to go to," he whispered in her ear. "As long as you come right back here when you're done."

"Do you think Santa Claus is going to be able to find us in California?" Carrie asked.

Kelly slid a tray of gingerbread men into the Holloways' oven and straightened up, removing her oven mitt. It was a week before Christmas, Hope was having its first light snowfall, and she was spending the evening baking holiday treats with the girls. Garth was outside gathering firewood. The whole house smelled like fresh pine thanks to the ten-foot tree the kids had picked out at a local Christmas tree farm. Between Christmas cookies, never-ending choruses of "Frosty the Snowman," and paper-cutout snowflakes, Kelly was definitely catching the holiday fever. It was hard for her to realize that in a few days she would be basking in the tropical sun.

Her cruise seemed strangely unreal.

She gave Carrie a quick hug. "I think Santa will find you no matter where you are," she said.

Julia had finally sent the tickets for their trip west. Kelly knew it was a huge relief to Garth that his girls wouldn't be disappointed again.

"Is he going to find you in the Carib— How do you say that again?" Carrie asked.

Kelly could see Michelle and Liza, sitting at the table with Toby, rolling their eyes at each other. The two older girls obviously thought themselves too old for Santa Claus stories.

"Caribbean," Kelly said. "I'm sure he'll find me. Don't worry."

"Where is the Caribbibbean?" Toby asked, stumbling over the word.

"Far away," Liza said.

Toby's eyes rounded. "How far? As far as China?"

"Do you know where China is?" Kelly asked.

"No. But it's far." Toby stared at her innocently.

Kelly laughed. "The Caribbean isn't as far as China. Next time you come over to my house, we'll go look at the globe, okay?"

She leaned down and switched on the oven light to check the gingerbread men through the glass window. They were puffy and golden, their little raisin eyes shining. She felt a sense of continuity. She remembered baking gingerbread men with her mother. With Brian and Bethany. Now new memories were being made—memories with Garth's children.

"Almost done." She turned around and saw Garth, framed in the doorway. He was wearing a jacket dusted lightly with snow. He pulled off his gloves. Her heart gave a little hitch, like it always did when he smiled at her.

"It sure smells great in here, ladies," he said, walking in. "Look at all these cookies!" Decorated sugar cookies cut in the shapes of Christmas trees and angels were cooling on the kitchen counters.

"Got enough firewood in?" Kelly asked.

Garth nodded. "Just about." He headed for the pantry, where from the top shelf he pulled down a small box that contained matches.

He'd already laid the fire, all the while catching snatches of his daughters' voices from the kitchen—singing Christmas carols, chattering, laughing. *There was happiness in his home.*

He palmed the matches and replaced the box on the top shelf. When he turned back around, Kelly was taking a tray of gingerbread men out of the oven. She placed the cookie sheet on the stovetop and reached up to sweep back a stray tendril that had escaped her French braid.

"Oooh!" the girls chorused, gathering around to poke at and admire the hot treats.

"Let them cool, girls," Kelly advised.

The scene—Kelly and his girls huddled by her side—shot straight to Garth's heart. He wanted to join them, to walk up behind Kelly and slide his arms around her waist. Then he wanted to kiss her, thank her for bringing light and life back into his world. He wanted to do it so badly that he forced himself to walk out of the room instead, to get the fire going. He'd made a point of downplaying his relationship with Kelly around the kids.

She was so good to his girls. And she was good to him. Good *for* him. She'd lifted him out of the bleak darkness he'd drifted into after the divorce. But Kelly had her own dreams. With the world calling her, could she ever be satisfied with a guy and four kids in Hope? She'd been honest enough to admit that she wasn't sure if she'd ever be ready to settle down.

It was important that they all keep their expectations in line with reality. The girls had been hurt too much already. So had he.

He lit a match, watched the fire blaze to life. Then he sat down on the couch, sweeping aside a sheet of paper. One of the kids' drawings. Carrie's name was in the top corner.

He picked it up. There were six figures and a dog in cheerful colors, standing in front of a house. Drawn in large childish forms, each figure had a name beneath it: Beast, Toby, Carrie, Michelle, Liza, Daddy . . . and Kelly.

They had sandwiches for dinner, followed by a round of Monopoly and another rehearsal of Carrie's lines for the next night's school play performance—then Garth sent the girls off to brush their teeth and get ready for bed. He sat on the couch with Kelly, the fire snapping and crackling in the grate.

"Are you and Kelly going to kiss now, after we go upstairs?" Michelle called from the foot of the stairs.

Garth craned his neck around and saw Toby, Carrie, and Liza waiting along with Michelle, all with obvious interest in his answer.

"That's none of your business," he said sternly. "Now upstairs with you." He made shooing motions with his hands and the girls pounded up the stairs, giggling.

He looked at Kelly.

"Well?" she prodded playfully, her blue eyes shining. "Are you going to kiss me now or what?"

She didn't sound bothered by Michelle's question. The kids seemed to view the idea of his kissing Kelly as funny too. Were they more capable of taking his relationship with Kelly in stride than he'd been giving them credit for? Or was that just wishful thinking?

He shook off the vague note of uncertainty. His moments alone with Kelly were too few and far between to waste. One day at a time, he reminded himself. He slid his arm around her back and pulled her closer.

"Yes," he said huskily. "I'm going to kiss you." And then he was through talking.

The next evening at the end of Carrie's play Kelly stood alongside Garth, clapping madly. The little girl, playing the princess in the elementary school's rendition of *Sleeping Beauty*, had been fabulous. She'd had her lines down pat, and her voice had been clear and confident. It was obvious she'd been having a ball center stage and loving it.

"She was wonderful!" Kelly cried over the roar in the auditorium. She turned to Garth. He put down the video camera for a moment and looked at her. His eyes were glowing with pride.

"She has her mother's talent," he said, then put his eye back to the viewfinder.

Kelly thought once more about what a deeply caring father Garth was. Julia had walked out on him, left him with four daughters, but he didn't display a bit of rancor in front of them. He encouraged Carrie's love of acting, even though it must be a bitter reminder to him of their mother. In all the time she'd spent with the Holloways, Kelly had never heard Garth speak an angry word about their mother in front of the girls.

The lights came on overhead. The curtain fell and Garth lowered the video camera. He'd taped the entire play. Carrie wanted to take it out to California with her to show to Julia.

They were scheduled to leave the next day. And so was Kelly.

They gathered the girls and headed backstage to pick up Carrie. The little girl was positively glowing.

"Daddy, Daddy, did you see me?" She ran up to her father, the material of her pink dress sparkling under the lights.

Garth chuckled. "Yes, sugar. I saw you. You were the best! The very best!" He picked her up and swung her around. "I'm so proud of you."

"Yeah, you were good, squirt," Liza added.

Kelly gave Carrie a kiss. "You looked beautiful," she told her. The little girl beamed.

For just a second the thought flashed through Kelly's mind of how much Carrie's mother was missing. No videotape could make up for being there, on the spot, to see the shine in Carrie's eyes, to be by Garth's side, to be part of the loving bond of family.

Then they were heading for the parking lot and the girls were all talking at once. Garth had ordered a cake from the bakery to celebrate Carrie's special night.

The kids barreled into the house through the garage entrance, heading through the living room and straight for the kitchen. The cake was decorated with pink and white icing with "Congratulations, Carrie" written across the middle in swirly script, the corners festooned with fat, creamy roses.

"Daddy! Hurry up!" Michelle called when Garth didn't come into the kitchen right away.

Kelly, standing in the doorway between the kitchen and the living room, watched as Garth stopped by the phone. The red light was blinking on the answering machine. He pressed the button.

"Girls, it's Mom."

Kelly froze, realizing that she was hearing Julia's voice for the first time. She wasn't sure what she'd expected, if she'd expected anything. The voice was a little husky and soft.

She sensed the girls coming up behind her, drawn by the sound of their mother's voice. They were suddenly silent.

Garth stared down at the phone.

"I'm sorry to have to do this, but I'm going to have to cancel your trip," Julia went on.

Kelly didn't hear most of the rest of it. The kids were already crying. Julia was saying something about a movie shoot in Toronto, that her schedule had changed, that she had to leave immediately. She hoped they could arrange a trip out during spring break instead.

"No, Mommy!" Carrie ran to the phone, grabbing the receiver as if she thought her mother might still be there. Garth caught the little girl, holding her tight as she sobbed.

Tears streamed down Michelle's face. Toby stuck her thumb in her mouth, her eyes huge. Liza crossed her arms tight across her chest.

The pain in the room was tangible. Kelly

looked at Garth. Her heart took an anguished beat as she saw the dark, haunted shadows in his face.

"I want to call Mommy," Michelle pleaded.

"I don't think she's at home right now," Garth explained. "She said she had to leave right away."

The gentleness in his voice was laced with controlled anger, simmering just beneath the surface.

Carrie tore herself out of his arms. "I want to see Mommy! She sent tickets. Can we go to Tor—Tor—"

"Toronto," Kelly supplied, feeling helpless to do more.

"Can we go to Toronto?" Carrie finished fretfully.

"No, sweetheart," Garth said. "You can't do that."

"Stop it, Carrie. Just stop it. Don't you get it?" Liza burst out suddenly, sharply. "She doesn't want us!" Tears slipped down her cheeks. She turned and flew up the stairs. There was no sound for a moment but the hitching of the girls' breaths between sobs and the slamming of Liza's bedroom door.

"Doesn't Mommy still love us, Daddy?" Carrie cried.

Kelly could feel her heart breaking.

"Sweetheart, yes, your mother loves you," Garth said softly. He reached out and took Carrie's hand.

The girl stared at him, her big brown eyes filled with hurt and confusion. "Then why doesn't she want to be with us for Christmas?" She didn't wait for her father to answer. She ran to Kelly. "Will you be with us for Christmas, Kelly? Can we come to your house like we did for Thanksgiving? Please!"

"Yes, please, Kelly," Michelle joined in.

"Oh, girls." Kelly put her arms around both of them. "I told you, I'm going away."

Garth stepped in. "We'll have Christmas here, girls. At our house."

But Carrie was already pushing away from Kelly's arm. "You don't have to leave," she cried. "You don't want us either!" She ran from the room.

"Carrie, that's not true." Kelly let go of Michelle and started to go after Carrie.

"No! Wait." Garth grabbed her arm and stopped her. "Michelle, Toby, go upstairs. I'll come up and talk to you in a little while."

Wiping at her cheeks, Michelle took Toby's hand and led her little sister out of the room.

Kelly pulled her arm from Garth. "I have to talk to Carrie—"

"Why? Are you going to tell her she can spend Christmas at your house?"

Stunned, Kelly stared at him.

"She wants someone to be there for her," he went on roughly, bitterly. "They all do. And God knows that someone isn't going to be their mother." He broke off, spun around, and paced several steps, then jerked his hand through his hair.

There was a tense silence.

"I'm sorry." He turned back. "I'm angry at Julia, not you."

"I told the girls about my trip weeks ago."

"I know." He closed his eyes for a brief moment, then opened them, staring at her with eyes that were dark, hollow. "This isn't your fault. It's mine. I've been selfish."

"You're the least selfish person in the world."

"No. You're wrong about that." He paced back to her. "The girls are fragile. So fragile. I thought they could handle this—us—but it's obvious they can't."

"They're upset about their trip being canceled." Her heart thumped in her chest. Suddenly she was scared, really scared. His eyes were so bleak. All the warmth and light and hope were gone. "That's natural."

"Yes. And it's also natural for them to turn to you when they're upset. These past weeks you've become like part of the family. They love you, Kelly."

"I love them too," she told him, feeling choked.

"But you're not ready to be a mother, are you? And that's how they're starting to see you."

Silence stretched between them. Kelly blinked, tried to speak, but words wouldn't come. She didn't know what to say. Confusion spun through her.

"You have this list of wonderful, exciting places to go to and things to do. You need time and space and I could give them to you, but the girls don't have the emotional maturity to understand that."

"What are you saying?" she asked.

He was quiet for long seconds before he spoke again. "I'm saying we need to pull back." His back was stiff, his face immobile. "The girls are starting to depend on you, to need you—too much."

"I would never hurt them," Kelly cried.

"Not on purpose." His words hung between them for what felt like forever. "But they're hurting right now. And you're not to blame for that," he went on quickly, "but it's happening just the same. You have your dreams, and I can't wish them away. But I can't wish the girls' needs away either. I can't bring someone into their lives who isn't ready to be there full time. And I can't ask you to be there full time, to settle down with us. You might regret giving up your dreams and blame me—"

"I'm not Julia," she said forcefully. "I would never walk out on a commitment."

"I know," he said quietly. "But I can't live with the fear that one day you'll wake up and I'll look across the breakfast table at you and know that you're sorry."

Kelly wanted to tell him he was wrong, but how could she be sure? What if he did ask her to settle down and she did wake up one day and regret giving up the dreams she'd longed for all these years?

What about the plans she'd spent her whole life making? Could she really let them go? She felt ripped apart inside. She didn't know what she wanted anymore.

She didn't want to cry, but first one tear, then another, rolled down her cheeks.

Garth made a strangled sound. "I don't want to hurt you." Then he was holding her. "I never meant to do that. I thought we could take it slow, find some in-between place that would be right for all of us, but that's not going to happen." His eyes shimmered with pain and defeat. "I should have stayed away from you, but I couldn't. No matter how impossible it was, I couldn't help . . ."

"What?" she whispered, staring up at him, needing him to finish, needing to hear what was in his heart.

"I couldn't help loving you."

And before she could speak, he closed his mouth over hers, kissing her with all the longing and desperation that Kelly felt too. He crushed her against him, holding her, just holding her, as if he would never let her go. And then he did, the sounds of the girls crying upstairs tearing them apart.

"I have to go to them," he whispered against her lips.

She nodded. She forced her trembling legs to move, to turn and walk away from him. Outside, into the cold darkness.

# FOURTEEN

The lights were magnificent. Tiny, clear white lights. A million of them, or so it seemed to Kelly through the blur of tears in her eyes.

The house was dark except for the Christmas tree lights. She'd been sitting on her couch—for how long, she wasn't certain—just staring at the tree, thinking about Garth and the girls and all the pain she was supposed to walk away from, not do anything about.

She wasn't sure why she'd put her tree up this year. The twins weren't going to be there and neither was she. But she'd put it up anyway, just because she'd done it every year and somehow it didn't seem right not to. It was her parents' tree, an artificial one circa 1960.

It was a rather ugly tree, but Kelly hadn't replaced it in the six years since her parents' death, even though when she was a teenager she'd always said that she hated it, wished her parents would buy a real one. But her mother had steadfastly refused. She had pictures of each of them as babies under it, and she wouldn't give up the tree for anything, even though some of the branches were permanently kinked out of shape from being stuffed into the box so many times.

So Kelly had kept it and decorated it every year with ornaments gathered over her parents' lifetime, some of them handmade. There was the paper angel she'd made in kindergarten, the crèche made of twigs Brian had picked up in the backyard, the twisted red and white pipe cleaners Beth had made into candy canes.

Kelly hadn't cried for her parents in a long time, and she wasn't sure whether she was crying for them now, or because this was the first year she wasn't going to spend the holidays with Brian and Beth, or because she knew there were four girls in the house next door who were crying too.

Upstairs, she had her suitcase out, and clothes in stacks on her bed. She needed to finish packing.

She thought about the cruise. The islands, the vivid blue of the Caribbean. The balmy breezes, the golden sun. It was all warm and bright, but it made her feel cold and dark instead.

Garth needed her. The girls needed her. She could heal them, she thought fiercely, her tears brimming anew. She loved them and they loved her. And that was everything that mattered, wasn't it?

*Do you think your parents were happy?* Garth had asked her once.

She'd spent so much time thinking about everything her parents had missed, she hadn't given much thought to everything they'd *had*. They'd had love—a home, a family. And an ugly old Christmas tree that Kelly was only now starting to see was beautiful because she finally understood what it had meant to her mother. It had meant love, a whole lifetime of it.

The kind of love she could share with Garth.

If he could trust her. If she could trust herself.

Garth flipped silver-dollar pancakes on the griddle. Christmas music played softly in the background.

A minute later he slipped the first one off the griddle and onto a waiting platter. Beast whined at his feet.

"All right, boy." Garth tossed the puppy a pancake, breaking his own no-people-food-for-dogs rule. "How is it? My cooking getting any better?" He'd only added water to a baking mix, so he was pretty sure he could manage.

The dog gobbled up the treat in one bite and wagged his little tail for more. Garth couldn't take the mutt's endorsement too seriously. Beast was just happy to be let inside on this bitterly cold Saturday morning.

It was early—the girls were still upstairs sleeping. Garth had tugged on a comfortable pair of old jeans and a thick sweatshirt and had headed downstairs to try to whip up a hearty breakfast before the girls got up. As if a hearty breakfast might somehow, just somehow, make them all feel better.

Snow was forecast for later in the day. If this weather kept up, maybe it would be a white Christmas. The kids would like that.

Garth was praying for a white Christmas. He was praying for anything that would help heal his girls' broken hearts.

They'd all had a long night. He'd spent hours talking to them, comforting them. And through all the pain, they were rebuilding. It wouldn't be easy, but that wasn't going to stop them.

He poured more batter onto the griddle. He felt wrung out. All his energy had been focused on comforting the girls. He had no comfort for himself, only weary acceptance. He'd done the right thing when he'd told Kelly to leave.

The right thing hurt. Kelly had opened his heart again, and he'd fallen in love with her. Deeply. Irrevocably.

But he couldn't ask her to stay, to give up her dreams. And he couldn't let things go on as they were, allowing the girls to grow emotionally dependent on someone who wasn't ready to settle down with a family.

Knowing all of that didn't make his heart ache one tiny bit less, though.

"Beast," he said, crouching down to scratch the puppy behind the ears, "keep your heart to yourself. No women. That's my advice."

The dog yipped in response and jumped up at the counter. Garth stood, sighed, and handed the mutt another pancake.

As he was flipping the pancakes, he heard the doorbell chime. "Jingle Bells" played softly on the stereo as he walked to the front door, the cheery tune in stark contrast to his heavy spirits.

It was awfully early for visitors, and he wasn't expecting anyone anyway. He pulled the door open and his heart stumbled, froze.

*Kelly.*

Kelly, with her spun-honey hair and her sky-blue eyes, stood on the stoop, wrapped in a bright red jacket—almost like a Christmas present.

He blinked, then stared. His chest tightened; his blood throbbed.

"Hi," she said softly. And she smiled, tremulously, shyly.

"What are you doing here?" he blurted out, only realizing after the words were out of his mouth how cold and rude they sounded.

Then he thought he understood. She was leaving for the airport, and Kelly, with her sensitive heart, was worrying about the girls. Her sweet, sensitive heart was going to be the death of him.

"The girls are all right, if that's why you're here," he said, cutting her off before she could answer his question. "We have a lot of work ahead of us, but we're going to be fine."

He needed her to stop worrying, stop being involved. They were neighbors, and seeing her from afar was going to be hard enough. She couldn't keep popping over. It would only make things harder. And things were hard enough. He had to make her understand that.

"That's not why I'm here," she said. "I mean, I'm glad to hear the girls are doing all right. But I'm not here about the girls. Well, they're part of it, of course. But I'm . . . uh . . ." She broke off nervously. "Do you mind if I come in? It's cold out here."

Garth stared at her, confused. "All right."

He let her in, closing the door behind her. She followed him into the kitchen, Beast yapping at her heels, trying to get her attention. Garth quieted the dog with another pancake.

He noticed his hands were shaking.

"Excuse me, I was making breakfast for the girls," he explained as he fixed his attention on the griddle, sliding the remaining pancakes off onto the waiting platter. He could hardly bear to look at Kelly. "They're still asleep," he said, filling the silence.

Finally he had to look at her again, his task completed. She was so beautiful. She watched him with a soft, tender expression, as if drinking the sight of him in. As if she couldn't get enough of him.

And he was sure he had to be imagining every bit of that.

"Don't you have a plane to catch?" he prompted gruffly. The longer she stood there, the more he was filled with a strange hope he couldn't justify. He needed her to leave, because hope hurt.

"I tried to go to the airport," she said. "I decided last night that I would try to go, to see if I *could* go. I made it as far as the end of the block. I was at the stop sign. I had everything—my ticket, my bags. But I just couldn't make myself go farther. Everything inside of me cried out to stay, so I drove around the block and came back.

"I've waited years for this chance," she rushed on when he would have interrupted her. "Years for the time when Brian and Beth would be old enough so that I would be free to do whatever I wanted. I'm free. Truly free . . . to go—or to stay."

"What do you mean?" He couldn't let himself hope, not yet, even though his heart felt as if it were pounding right out of his chest. Was he dreaming? Had he really gotten out of bed this morning?

Beast licked his bare feet, so he was pretty sure he was awake.

"I mean that I know I'll always dream of exotic, far-off places." Her eyes shone clear and true and certain. "Even so, I could live the rest of my life just fine without ever leaving Hope. But I can't live one more night without you."

"But it's your dream—"

"Last night I went through all our old photo albums," she went on. "I had forgotten how happy my parents were. They didn't miss out on anything they really wanted. They were where they wanted to be—with us.

"And when I looked at the pictures from the time after they died, from when I took over raising Brian and Beth, I saw things in there I had forgotten too. Oh, I hadn't forgotten some things, like how hard it was. I was so young and I felt so trapped. But I loved them, and we had good times. Lots of them. And I wouldn't have missed those times for anything. There was sacrifice, but there was also joy."

"But you're free now."

"Exactly. I'm free. You're not trapping me. You let me go, sent me away."

"I would never ask you to give up your freedom, your dreams, for us."

"You're not asking me. I'm asking you." Her voice wavered with emotion, and she steadied it. "I love you, Garth. And I love the girls too. I don't want to leave. I want to spend Christmas and New Year's and every other day between now and forever right here with you."

"But the world—"

"The world will wait. It will still be there later, when the kids grow up. I don't want the world anymore—not without you. I want to make new dreams. With you."

And then whatever else she was going to say was lost, muffled, as Garth made a soft, tortured sound in his throat and pulled her into his arms.

"I love you," he whispered against her hair. Then he drew back, put his hands on her face, touching her, feeling her. "Are you sure? You've got to be sure."

"I'm sure," she whispered, tears brimming in her eyes. "More sure than I've ever been of anything in my life. You don't have to wonder if I'll wake up one day and be sorry. I won't. The only thing I could ever regret would be leaving you."

"It won't be easy with the girls. They're going to be hurting for a long time."

"I know."

She met his gaze steadily, and Garth realized finally that he wasn't alone anymore. Wouldn't ever be alone again. He had Kelly. He had love.

He had everything.

"Kelly!"

Kelly spun around in Garth's arms and found Carrie in the doorway. She wore a long white flannel nightgown dotted with little purple flowers. Shyly, she entered the kitchen. Toby, Michelle, and Liza arrived behind her.

"Are you on your way to the airport, to your trip?" Carrie asked.

"No," Kelly told her. "I'm not going. I'm staying here for Christmas. If that's all right with all of you."

The girls' eyes rounded.

"I'm sorry I said mean things to you," Carrie said, gazing up at her with a worried expression.

"You were scared." Kelly bent and put her arms around her. "I know that."

"Will you cook the Christmas turkey?" Michelle asked. "Will you cook all the turkeys from now on?"

Kelly straightened, looked at Garth. His eyes glowed with laughter. A sudden rush of emotion, of love, for this family blurred her vision. They needed her, and she needed them. How had she ever thought she could leave, even for a second? She belonged there.

The certainty of her decision shimmered through to her soul. She thought of what Jenna had said earlier. She'd dashed into her own house before going to Garth's and called Jenna. She'd caught her friend on her way out the door to the airport. Jenna and Diane would be going on the cruise on their own. Jenna had told Kelly that she was the luckiest woman in the world. And Kelly had had to agree with her.

She was fabulously, blissfully lucky.

"Yes," she promised. "I'd like that."

"How does an engagement ring sound for Christmas?" Garth asked her, his voice husky.

He slid his arms around her again, sending shivers of remembered passion along with sweet promise for the future straight to her heart. She leaned against his chest, looking from him to the girls and back again. It all felt so very right, so magical and precious. Her heart was practically bursting.

"I think that sounds perfect," she said. "Absolutely perfect."

Liza gasped. "They're getting married!" she cried gleefully.

The girls let out whoops and ran into the living room, followed by Beast yapping excitedly behind them. Within seconds they were calling, "Daddy, Kelly!"

Together, Garth and Kelly walked to the doorway of the living room. The girls stood in the center of the room, staring at the Christmas tree.

Wrapped gifts were scattered on the floor.

"Oh, no," Garth breathed. He looked at Kelly. "I couldn't sleep last night," he whispered. "After I finally got the girls to bed, I brought some of their presents down from the attic to wrap. I forgot to take them back up. Thank goodness that's not *all* the gifts."

He walked up to the tree, to the girls, Kelly at his side.

"Can we open them?"

"Where did they come from?"

"Are they for us?"

The girls barreled out the questions, their eyes alight with excitement.

Garth looked at Kelly.

"Go ahead, girls," he said. He touched Kelly's face, stroking a tender caress across her cheek. And he smiled, a big, joyful smile. "Santa came early this year."

# THE EDITORS' CORNER

Ladies, step back! This July, LOVESWEPT is hotter than ever, with a month full of beguiling heroes and steamy romance. We managed to capture four Rebels with a Cause for your reading pleasure. There's Jack, a rough-and-tough detective with a glint in his eye; Luke, an architect who has to prove his innocence to win the heart of his woman; Clint, an FBI renegade with a score to settle; and Mitch, an ex-Navy Seal who's determined to earn back the life he left behind.

Beautiful Alex Sheridan and sexy Luke Morgan pack a lifetime of passion into **JUST ONE NIGHT**, LOVESWEPT #898, Eve Gaddy's sexy tale of two strangers who are trying to forget the past. As an officer on the Dallas bomb squad, Alex is called in to investigate the bombing of a construction site. All leads point to Luke, the architect on the project: he's a trained explosives expert; a large amount of money mysteriously shows up in his account; *and* he's the son of a convicted terrorist. As the hunt for the bomber continues, Alex and Luke are in too deep to keep their relationship on a professional basis. Alex had feared she'd never be able to trust herself again, but will Luke convince her that her instincts about him are right? Eve Gaddy pulls at the heartstrings in this moving story of a man who's backed against a wall and the woman who's willing to risk everything to save him.

In **A SCENT OF EDEN,** LOVESWEPT #899, Cynthia Powell demonstrates the delicious power of unlikely attractions. When Eden Wellbourne's fiancé goes missing, it's up to her to find the culprit. To that end, she hires Jack Rafferty, a man who is reputed to have an unmatched expertise in locating missing persons, a man who is clearly living on the edge. Meanwhile, Jack is having the second-worst day of his life, and he's definitely not in the mood to deal with the uptown girl standing on his doorstep. With his cash flow at an all-time low, however, he reluctantly decides to take on her case. Both are confused at the physical pull they feel toward each other, but neither wants to act on it first. When a break-in convinces Eden her own life is in danger, she turns to Jack for more than just his people-finding talents. Everything comes up roses when Cynthia Powell crosses a down-on-his-luck tough guy with a perfume princess.

Next, Jill Shalvis offers **LOVER COME BACK,** LOVESWEPT #900. As the editor of the *Heather Bay Daily News*, Justine Miller makes it her business to know what's happening in her town. But nothing could have prepared her for the shock of seeing her long-lost husband again. Not to mention the fact that he's the proud new owner of her newspaper. Two years earlier, Justine had anxiously waited for her new husband to return to their honeymoon suite. Only, Mitch Conner had disappeared, leaving Justine to deal with the embarrassment and pain. Mitch had had no choice but to leave her, but now he's back and more than eager to reclaim the love of his life. Justine refuses to believe his cockamamy story of corruption and witness protection programs. She has had her taste of marriage and love, and she's through with it. Mitch faces the toughest assignment of his life—proving to her that he'll never leave her. Jill Shalvis delivers a story of true love that can stand the test of time.

Finally, Karen Leabo brings us **THE DEVIL AND THE DEEP BLUE SEA,** LOVESWEPT #901. FBI agent Clint Nichols has a plan. Not a well-thought-out plan, but a plan nonetheless. He's going to kidnap a sister to exchange for an ex-wife. But the minute he boards the *Fortune's Smile*, Clint knows this mission will be a bust. His pretty quarry, Marissa Gabriole, pulls a gun on him and his getaway boat sinks. He's also hampered by a hurricane on the way and an accomplice who's a moron. Marissa soon grows tired of being on the run and chooses to team up with her kidnapper to flush out a mob boss. Clint isn't sure whether he can trust Marissa, but he knows it's the only way to wrap up an extensive undercover operation. Besides, what more does he have to lose? His life, for one thing. His heart, for another. Karen Leabo expertly blurs the line between what's right and what's love in this fast-paced, seaworthy caper.

Happy reading!

*Susann Brailey*    *Joy Abella*

Susann Brailey              Joy Abella

Senior Editor               Administrative Editor